I0629840

OCTOBER FIRE

Books in the Mackenzie Prentice Mysteries Series

October Fire
Buried in Treasure
Painted Lady
On the Edge
Old Habits
My Cousin Krissy
Mack on Ice (2026)

OCTOBER FIRE

A MACKENZIE PRENTICE MYSTERY

MARY PIERCE

Seven Windows LLC

Copyright © 2023 by Mary Pierce.

All rights reserved.

ISBN 979-8-9881776-6-1

Published by Seven Windows LLC

No part of this publication may be reproduced, distributed, or transmitted in any form or by any means, including photocopying, recording, or other electronic or mechanical methods, without the prior written permission of the publisher, except as permitted by U.S. copyright law. For permission requests, contact infosevenwindowsllc@gmail.com.

The story, all names, characters, and incidents portrayed in this production are fictitious. No identification with actual persons (living or deceased), places, buildings, and products is intended or should be inferred.

Cover Art Concept by Geri Krause (www.gerikrause.com; Instagram: @gerikrause)
Book Design by Michelle Rayburn (www.missionandmedia.com)

First edition 2023

For my father who believed
and Gladys who dreamed

Sunday, October 28

Seven days after I heard Billy was dead, I stood on the street at midnight, watching what was left of my pathetic life go up in smoke. Bad end to a bad week. Someone was upset with all the snooping I'd been doing. I wasn't sure who. All I knew at that moment was someone wanted me to stop and wanted it badly enough to try and kill me.

CHAPTER ONE

Sunday, October 21, 6:42 p.m.

MY GRANDMOTHER SAYS THAT trouble comes in threes. Based on recent events, I say trouble comes in fours, fives, and sometimes sixes.

I stood before the bathroom mirror, massaging purple goo into my hair. I'd selected Miss Lovely's Cinnamon Toffee hair color to get rid of the way-too-soon-to-have-them-at-thirty-five gray hairs. A couple blobs landed on the bathroom counter, but I didn't care. The bathroom is a wreck, like the rest of this apartment, a lower duplex where I've lived for the past year. Nothing's been renovated since the 1960s. Some people are crazy about the mid-century modern look, but this turquoise and pink bathroom is mid-century disaster.

I hoped a change of hair color—from mousy brown to Cinnamon Toffee—would perk up the romance with my latest boyfriend, a computer geek named Kyle I'd been seeing for three months. Kyle said he wanted to "take it slow," and so far, we'd only held hands.

My cell phone buzzed. Caller ID said "Stella." My ex-mother-in-law. Billy and I had been divorced a year, which was two years after we separated, which was ten years after we got married, but who's counting.

Jim and Stella Stone live in the little town of Deerwood, a couple hours to the north of the bigger town of Three Rivers, where I live. Hadn't seen them in ages. Why hadn't I deleted the in-laws' number? A shrink might say I had some subconscious desire to reconcile with Billy. I say I'd been busy moving on with my life and hadn't noticed it was still there. I made a mental note to delete it later.

I tapped "speaker" with my right plastic-gloved pinky knuckle, trying not to gunk up the phone. Another purple blob plopped to the counter. A near miss. "Hello?"

"Mackenzie? Is that you?"

"Hey, Stella."

"Oh God, Mackenzie, it's been so long since we talked," she started. *Right, Stella. We might have been talking more regularly if you didn't hate me and hadn't accused me of stealing.*

I offered a mild, "Mmm, hmmm."

She let out a long sigh. "William . . ." she said, and I felt my hackles rise. Stella always insisted on calling Billy "William." He hated that. He'd always preferred Billy, as in Billy the Kid, gunslinger. Badass Billy the Cop.

Billy. Not William, as Stella insisted. Maybe this was just a typical conflict between mother-in-law and daughter-in-law. Which hen rules the roost? Stella had been annoying. I said "Billy," and she said "William." Every. Dang. Time.

She sucked in a breath. "I'm calling to let you know that William is dead."

A drip of cold goo traced down the back of my neck.

Trouble numero uno.

I swallowed hard. "Hang on a sec." I stripped off the plastic gloves, going out of speaker mode as I walked out into the living room. My throat felt tight as I sank onto my ancient couch. "Billy's dead?"

"Yes. They found him—" She cleared her throat. "They found him near here, in that cabin he rented from his uncle Eddie. You remember Jim's brother Eddie, don't you?"

I gave a quick "uh-huh," and she continued. "He was . . . he'd been . . ." She stopped again.

My stomach knotted. My mind raced. *Been what? Drinking? Doing drugs? Both? Overdose? Shot himself? Accident? On purpose?* Just some of the options for how Billy might have wound up dead. He had been a cop in Three Rivers when we were married. He had a gun. He drank a lot in the past and had messed around with drugs too. He had the means. Maybe he'd found a reason.

I broke the silence. "He'd been what, Stella?"

I heard her suck in a big gulp of air. "They say it was an overdose. But you know that old cabin just has that wood stove. Remember? You and William used to go there. Maybe it was carbon monoxide. I don't know. Who knows for sure? And that's the hardest thing, not knowing." She fell silent again.

I'd spent plenty of time since we split imagining how we'd end up. I'd be living happily ever after—naturally—and Billy would end up with some ho-bag, like the ones he cheated on me with, who would make his life a living hell. Or he'd end up alone, addicted to something, living out his years miserable and sorry he ever let me go. I never imagined he'd be dead. I was supposed to have both our lifetimes to watch him be miserable while I lived the good life. I felt cheated. Again.

Stella continued. "They say it was an overdose, but I don't

think—no, I *know* it wasn't. No, it couldn't have been." Trying to convince herself. "William goes to AA meetings, and he isn't taking any more of those drugs. I mean, he went . . . Things were getting so much better, or so we thought . . ." She trailed off again.

So. Billy was dead. What did I feel? Sad? Yes. But frankly, I'd been too mad at him to miss him much. Mostly I felt numb.

"I'm sorry, Stella, sorry for you and Jim." Billy was their only child. "Is there anything I can do?" I figured there was nothing she wanted from me, so I could be the bigger person and at least offer.

"That's why I'm calling. There are some things here for you. Things William—uh, things he left behind." She sighed. "I can't believe he's gone. It's just been such a shock. Just the other day—"

I interrupted her. "When is the funeral?"

Tuesday. Bigelow Funeral Home in Deerwood. Visitation at eleven, and the service at noon. "I hope you'll come. William would want you there."

Would he? Would I want me there? The knot in my stomach got bigger as a battle raged in my head. Wounded ex-wife still angry at the cheating jerk versus decent human being who could forgive and move on. Decent Me won. "Okay. I'll come."

I assured her again how sorry I was for her loss. "It's your loss too," she said. She was right, of course.

I told her I'd see her on Tuesday and hung up. The couch springs creaked as I slumped back. I sat there for several minutes. Billy. Gone. Loss. What did I feel? Numbness and a weird kind of matter-of-factness, like, "Okay, someone I used to know is gone." Did I feel nothing more than that for the man with whom I'd shared years of my life?

I looked toward the living room window. The sun had set, and the town had gone dark. The streetlight in front of the apartment building streaked the hardwood floor. Then I remembered the purple goo.

"Geez Louise!" I yelled at Tweet and Chirp, my two blue parakeets. "Geez Louise!" is one of my eighty-year-old grandmother's favorite expressions. In reply, Tweet offered a chirp. And Chirp added a tweet. Or maybe it was the other way around. They look a lot alike.

I ran to the bathroom, wriggled the plastic gloves back on. (Why is it so hard to put those things back on once you take them off?) I bent over the sink and used a paper cup to rinse the dye out of my hair. The instructions warned me not to shampoo for three days, lest I undo all the processing. I hoped I wasn't going to have another hair disaster.

I started DIY hair coloring in ninth grade. The first time, I ended up with a weird combo of pink and green. You'd think I'd have quit then, but another time, when I was going for a few blonde highlights, I ended up with one huge white streak, a la Bride of Frankenstein. *Tres chic.*

Some girls seem to float through life effortlessly, looking great and attracting love and success without so much as lifting a precious pinky. I'm not that gal. I've had to work at everything I've achieved, not that I've achieved much.

One failed marriage. A mediocre job. A crappy apartment. A bachelor's degree in psychology, which everyone knows doesn't qualify you for much. A so-so relationship. A so-so life.

Average. Average life. Average me. At five-foot-six, I'm not too tall, not too short, not too fat, not too thin. A Goldilocks "just-right" kind of girl.

My just-rightness had been just right for Billy. We met in high school. The bad-boy son of the wealthy Stones, he came to live with his aunt in Three Rivers after he was expelled from Deerwood High.

Billy sat behind me in geometry class. I liked the way the back of my neck tingled when he leaned forward to whisper, "What did you get for number six?"

We clicked right away. We both loved hamburgers with mustard and extra pickles. And vintage Frankenstein-era horror movies. I guess that helped when I had the white-streak hair disaster.

Yes, Billy and I connected in all the important ways—hamburgers and horror movies. Enough to build a lifetime of happiness on. That's the adolescent mind, right? Thinking those things matter and are enough. That's what you think with your first love. You think it's going to last forever. And sometimes it does.

Ours didn't.

CHAPTER TWO

Monday, October 22

I WHIMPERED A LITTLE AT the first glance in the mirror the next morning. My hair stood up in all directions, a mass of multi-toned, reddish, brownish—and even some pinkish—clumps. I looked like an angry striped squirrel who'd maybe stuck a paw in an electrical outlet. That call from Stella had messed things up.

Since I had to get to work, I looked for a hat to see if I could disguise the disaster. A jaunty fedora would have been perfect. If I owned one, which I didn't. And if I could pull off "jaunty." Which I could not.

A stocking cap pulled down to my eyes gave me a sinister look. I could end up on the news. *Angry squirrel robs bank! Film at eleven!*

I finally opted for a scarf that I tied in what I thought was a lovely little knot, slightly off-center above my right eyebrow. At first glance, I looked stylish. At second glance, I looked dumb. I took it off, shook out my hair, and smoothed it down as much as I could. It would just have to do. *Give it up.*

I headed to the kitchen and gave the last of the milk the sniff test. It passed. I slopped it into the last of my granola and ate it on the living room couch, watching the local TV news and weather.

There's never really much news in Three Rivers, an all-American, apple pie, Fourth of July kind of town of 20,000, give-or-take, with little crime and a friendly feel. Big enough that everybody isn't busy with everybody else's business but small enough that when I'm out and about, I see people I know. Kids from school. Friends of our family. Old neighbors.

We have four seasons here in the north country, each with its own beauty, its own treachery. This October felt weird. This time of year, approaching Halloween, we would normally be hunkering down with chilly, drizzly days. But summer-like warmth, and the drought we'd had since July, continued. The wind had a gritty feel.

The weather, always a big topic of conversation, was especially so this year. "Looks like we're having another warm one." "Yup. No telling when it'll end." "Whew, like the Sahara around here!" "Ya know, if I'd wanted this, I'd have moved to Arizona!"

Today, the morning weather guy on our one television station predicted "another day with above-average temps, unseasonably warm, with no rain in sight."

No news. No change in the weather. Same-old, same-old. I shut off the TV, rinsed my bowl, and gave Tweet and Chirp fresh water and seed, promising them I'd clean their cage after work. I told them to keep an eye on the apartment and locked the back door.

As I drove my ten-minute commute, I made a mental note to let Kyle know I'd be out of town on Tuesday. I wondered if I should ask Kyle to come to the funeral. Were we a casual-dating couple or a go-to-a-wedding-together couple? A go-to-the-ex-husband's-funeral couple? Were we even a couple? I didn't know. Mental note two: figure that out.

Note three: call my mother on my lunch hour. My mother had moved us five kids—I'm the lucky middle child—here to Three Rivers, a couple of hours' drive from "The City" where I was born. I'd just started middle school. My father had left one night to get cigarettes and never came back. My mom waited a year, then divorced him, and we moved.

Three Rivers is where Mom grew up and where most of our extended family lives. My mother said it was a good place to start over, that The City was no place to raise five kids, especially as a single mother. She was probably right. We all turned out pretty well.

The sun was bright in the blue October sky as I parked in the municipal lot on River Street. I stopped for a moment, looking across the Wolf River, the largest of the three rivers that converge here—hence the town's name.

Decades ago, some local students carved a huge "3R" into the cliff on the far side of the Wolf. As the story goes, they did this after a broken-hearted classmate nose-dived to her death from the top of the cliff. Jumped or pushed? Who knows? No one ever figured that one out, and whoever had answers is long gone.

Every town has its mysteries. Was Billy's death going to be one of Deerwood's? What happened? Was it an accidental over-dose? Or suicide? Or something else entirely?

I inhaled the warm, dry morning air and walked the half-block to my friend Tansy's yoga studio on the ground floor of a gorgeous old brownstone. The building once housed the first bank in town. Tansy offers a 7:00 a.m. "Morning Stretch" class, and the last two women were leaving as I walked in.

Tansy Pemberley and I met in sixth grade—she was my first friend when we moved to Three Rivers. Her family is rich. I mean, R-I-C-H rich. The kind of rich where you never have to stop to ask, "Can I afford this?" because, well, you can always afford it. That dinner entrée? Sure. That designer dress? No sweat. That Ferrari? Not a problem.

And even though Tansy grew up in the lap of luxury and I grew up on luxury's backside, we hit it off right away as soon as we realized we both had brothers who bugged us.

One day in middle school, Tansy offered to pay for my lunch on a day I forgot mine at home. I told her if we were going to be friends, she couldn't do that. When she asked why, I said, "I know you have more money than God." (I knew that was true because my mother had said at dinner one night, "Those Pemberleys have more money than God.")

I went on. "But reminding me that you're rich and I'm not by offering to pay feels crappy. So, knock it off." Tansy knocked it off, and we've been best friends ever since.

She is the kind of friend who'll back me up. I can tell her how so-and-so said such-and-such to me, and she will be as angry as I am. "How dare they say that to you?" she'll say. Some people say they want a best friend who will be honest with them—tell them the truth even if it's hard to hear. I disagree. I want a friend who will side with me, even when I'm being ridiculous. Because I know when I'm being ridiculous, and I'll come around. But in that moment, I just need a friend. Tansy Pemberley is that kind of friend.

This morning, Tansy looked so awake my eyes hurt to look at her. Her neon-pink stretchy tank top hugged her athletic body above pink and yellow print leggings. She was barefoot, as usual. As a final flourish, she'd twisted a fluorescent yellow headband around the blonde bun atop her head.

Tansy colors her hair like I do. Well, not actually like I do because she can afford to make a trip to The City every month or so and comes back with a professional style. Sometimes she has blue, green, or fuchsia highlights—all there on purpose. What Tansy does with her hair is always intentional and a delightful surprise. My hair surprises are never delightful.

Tansy finished rolling up her yoga mat as I approached. She smiled. "Hey, Mack. I was going to call you later." She noticed my hair. "Whoa! Interesting new look."

When my eyes filled with tears, her smile turned to concern. "Oh gosh. I'm sorry. Your hair looks great." Sometimes the best friends are the best liars.

I sniffed. "It's not that." I told her about Billy.

Tansy said, "Oh, Mack, I'm so sorry! You were a great couple, you know, before . . ."

I nodded. "We *were* great, weren't we, until . . . yeah. Well, you know when you're divorced, you focus on all the bad stuff that happened. You hang on to the hurt," I said.

"Yes, of course you do," Tansy said.

"You hang on to the hurt so you can tell yourself there are good reasons you're alone. You tell yourself that."

Tansy nodded.

I swallowed hard and continued, the words coming in a rush against the press of tears. "But then they die, you realize you never stopped loving them, but suddenly there is no possibility of ever getting back together, and you realize that you've spent years wishing for exactly that!" The dam burst. Between gulping sobs, I said, "All this time . . . I just wanted him to . . . come to his senses . . . say he was sorry and come back. I just wanted him to come . . . back . . ."

"Of course, you did," Tansy said, holding me tight. "And he would have, I'm sure."

She hugged me for several minutes while I cried. When I'd calmed, she released me and offered me a box of tissues. I dried my tears and blew my nose. She hugged me again.

"You going to be okay?"

I nodded and sniffed. "I hope so."

She offered to come to the funeral with me. I thanked her but assured her I'd be fine going it alone. She told me to let her know if there was anything she could do. That's what people always say in a bad time, but I knew Tansy meant it.

I hugged her one more time, told her I'd call her later, and headed off to work, feeling better.

As Gram says, "A burden shared is a burden halved." She's right.

CHAPTER THREE

KIPLING FINANCIAL IS ON River Street, on the second floor of what used to be First Savings Bank back in the days before the savings and loan industry melted down. Kipling Financial is owned by "Big George" Kipling, whose family fortune came from lumber, like most of Three Rivers' founding families. Big George drops by the office every month or so just to check up on his son, George the Third, who goes by "Trip," as in Triple. Trip is my boss.

Trip is a couple years older than I am. We might have been in school together, except that, as the son of a rich man, Trip went to private schools. I'd heard of the Kipling family while growing up, of course. The Kiplings and the Pemberleys are among the upper crust in our little town. But until I came to work here, I'd never actually met Trip.

I wouldn't call Trip incompetent, but let's just say he's not the sharpest tool in the shed. Big George conducts most of the business, which is offering financial advice to the wealthy.

Trip is just a place-keeper, as in keeping the place open. What Trip does is whatever Big George has him doing, and I'm just Trip's lackey—with the politically correct title of administrative assistant. I take phone messages, make copies, do a little filing, water the plants, and make coffee on the rare occasion a client or anyone else important is coming by.

I don't do anything that Trip himself couldn't be doing but having me do it sustains his image as the big-shot financial executive who has "people" (meaning yours truly) to do the grunt work while he plays golf. The job is a no-brainer. I can go home at night and forget about it.

Past plans to expand the office and hire more financial advisors and maybe another support person never panned out. And lately, things have been quiet. Very quiet. Even the plants look like they're giving up.

Back to Monday morning. I made it to work at 8:25. I'm supposed to be there at eight on-the-dot, but the hair thing this morning and talking to Tansy slowed me down. The office door opens to a small waiting area with a cubicle behind a half-wall, where I sit as the receptionist-slash-flunky.

"A gal Friday," Gram says.

My mother chimes in, "Mackenzie, you're underemployed. You have a college degree. Why are you settling?" My mother is constantly reminding me that I "deserve better."

I remind her that my psychology degree qualifies me for not much and that Three Rivers is not The City, and I feel lucky to be working at all.

I unlocked the office and plopped down at my desk. I took the little mirror out of my desk drawer and checked my face for post-sob damage. Not too puffy. No mascara streaks on cheeks.

I shoved my purse into the bottom drawer.

My desk faces the front door. To my left are three offices. Two are empty; the one closest to me is Trip's office. Next to his door is a wall of glass. I can see everything that goes on in there.

Trip's office was empty. Lights off. *Kind of like the man himself,* Snarky Me snarked.

Nice Me countered with, *Cut him some slack. He's been living in his old man's shadow his whole life.* Yup. I do have my moments of empathy and generosity of spirit.

I'd been at my desk less than fifteen minutes, looking for online bargains, when Trip arrived wearing a sweatshirt and jeans instead of his usual shirt, tie, and sportscoat. He hadn't shaved, and his tousled dark hair had a bad case of bedhead. He plowed past me, head down, grumbling to himself. Not the right moment to tell him about Billy and that I'd need the next day off for the funeral.

"Good morning to you too," I called after him.

He grunted something, flipped on his office lights, and slammed his door. Looking over my cubicle wall, I saw him on his cell phone, his face twisted, his free arm going fifty miles an hour as he yelled. After a couple of minutes, he threw his cell down on the desk, opened the office door, and hollered, "Mack! Come in here!" Like I was fifty feet away instead of three.

He paused when he realized I hadn't jumped at his command. I leaned back in my chair, folded my arms, and stared at him. After a few beats in which I watched him visibly deflate, he added, "Please?"

In the time I've worked for Trip, I've made a concerted effort to teach him some manners. At first, he was like one of those spoiled little chihuahuas you see on TV; the dog trainer on the show comes in to teach the chihuahua to stop growling and snapping at people.

I'd done my own training with Trip, refusing to respond to his rude commands, teaching him that polite adults use "please" and "thank you" in interactions with other humans.

I stood and walked into his office and sat in one of his comfy chairs, which was way comfier than any other chair in my sad little life. Trip closed the door, then sat at his desk.

He looked at me, tears brimming. *Tears?* This was new. I waited. He fiddled with the papers on his desk, then said, "I have some news. It's not good." His tears overflowed. I looked away. We sat for a while, him silent and me staring at my shoes until I heard him blow his nose and clear his throat.

"Ha! Bet you never expected to see me do that, huh?" He'd read my mind. Then he noticed my hair. "What the hell happened to your hair?"

"Long story," I said. "But what's going on, Trip?"

"I talked to Big George this morning." Yes, even his son calls him that. "He's doing some restructuring, making cutbacks . . ." His voice trailed off.

I waited as long as I could. "Cutbacks? You mean like fewer staples?" A feeble attempt to lighten the moment.

"No. Like fewer people."

My stomach knotted. "Like which people?"

"Like me," he said, staring down at his desk, then adding after a few beats, "and like you."

I said nothing, just sat there with that feeling that life has changed and you don't have a clue what's going to happen next, but you know nothing good is coming. Trip's words hung in the office like cold, dank fog.

"You mean I'm fired," I said at last.

"Well, yeah, but I am too!" He shook his head. "He's closing the office. How is this happening? After all I've done for that old . . ." He ranted on, spewing stuff about his "old man" and how much he'd sacrificed for his father and Kipling Financial.

Trip mewled on about the terrible turn his life had taken, clueless that, comparatively speaking, he would still be the son and heir of a wealthy man. He'd still have his sports car and his vacation home and his lovely rich-boy life. That, no doubt, helped soothe the sting of being fired by your own father.

Trip still had his life, while I, on the other hand, would be completely and utterly screwed. Unable to make rent on my crappy apartment, I'd wind up living under a bridge somewhere.

I asked, "So when is this happening?"

"Today. Now. Pack your stuff. Big George says he'll send you a check, you know, for the rest of the pay period."

I stood, trying to figure out what to say. "Well. All righty, then," was all I could manage. I walked out of his office, leaving him muttering about the blankety-blank internet and how it had ruined the financial services business and how nobody appreciated face-to-face service anymore.

Feeling numb, I went to the storeroom, got a box, and cleared out the few personal items I had in my cubicle. Packed up, I went to Trip's office door to say goodbye.

"Hey, Trip," I said, and he looked up. He was crying again. I knew from overhearing conversations between Trip and his dad that Big George considered him a miserable failure, but Trip wasn't such a bad guy. He just couldn't seem to measure up to Daddy's standards. I felt a little sorry for him.

Sympathetic Me said, "It's gonna be okay, Trip." He gave me a skeptical look and frowned. I went on. "And just so you know, it wasn't too horrible working for you." That made him start crying again. I felt another tiny twinge of pity. "Good luck, Trip."

He stopped what he was doing and came and hugged me. *Awkward.* He let go, stepped back, sniffed in hard, and cleared his throat. "Just so you know," he said, "you weren't the worst secre—" He corrected course. "Um, administrative assistant I've ever had." He sniffed again. "And hey, you never know. I've got some ideas cooking, and maybe we'll work together again. There's always hope, right?"

I stared at him. Snarky Me thought, *Does the poor, clueless dolt really think another job as his flunky is worth waiting around for, just in case? Heck, a gal Friday with my brains and good looks, to say nothing of this hair, could get a job flunking for someone else in a heartbeat.*

I didn't say any of that, of course. Nice Me said, "Sure, Trip. You gotta keep hope alive."

I went back to my desk, picked up my purse and my box of stuff, and at 9:27 a.m., I walked out, carrying trouble number two with me.

CHAPTER FOUR

I SWUNG BY LAMBERT'S GROCERY to pick up some vital household supplies while I still had a positive balance in my checking account. I grabbed tampons, toilet paper, toothpaste, shampoo, birdseed, milk, granola, and several kinds of candy. Like I said, vital supplies.

Sometimes I wonder if I have a sugar addiction, if such a thing actually exists. I assure myself I can quit anytime. I know that's true because I've done it—at least fifty times. And I know that scarfing boxes of Milk Duds doesn't make my problems disappear, but candy helps me forget for a minute that I have problems. Wine does the same thing, but with more regret the morning after.

I stopped at the ATM and got cash, which I'd need when I headed north for Billy's funeral. The account balance on the ATM receipt gave me pause—I had maybe a month and a half before I'd be begging on the street.

I texted Kyle and asked him to call me.

My phone chirped a few minutes later, just as I pulled into the parking space behind my apartment. Kyle. He'd just finished a bike ride and was at Rawley Park, the beautiful, sprawling acreage near downtown a few blocks from my place. He said he'd meet me in the parking lot. I backed out and drove to the spot.

Kyle had long-term potential. Tall, lean, and athletic, with clear green eyes and a nice smile. A couple of crooked teeth added to his charm. What more could a girl ask?

We had a bunch of stuff in common. He liked to cook; I liked to eat. He liked to fish; I liked to eat fish. He liked hiking, biking—in general, anything that was outside.

I don't mind being outside if it's not too cold. Or too hot. Or too humid. Or too buggy. Or too early. Or too late. Which means that here in Three Rivers, there's one day of the year, for about an hour and a half, when conditions are just right.

But I liked Kyle, so I pretended to like the hiking and biking, the kayaking and in-line skating, even though I truly sucked at everything except walking. My mother taught my sisters and me that if we wanted to have a boyfriend, we should be interested in what they were interested in, so I gave Kyle my best fake interest. But despite my best efforts, in our three months together, we'd never gotten past handholding. Taking it slow, for Kyle, meant glacier-slow.

I saw him and parked. He came to my car. "Let's take a walk," he said. We walked in silence while I tried to decide where to start. Billy dying, or me getting fired. We reached a bench facing the park's pond. Kyle sat and patted the seat beside him. "Sit down. I have to tell you something."

Uh-oh. That sounded like "we have to talk." My stomach did a flip-flop as that little voice in my head, Anxious Me, started up with, *Oh no. No. NO! Please don't break up with me. Things were going so well between us, I even pictured something longer term, like maybe six months, and this will turn out to be the worst day of my life if you dump me now.*

And then he did just that.

"I'm sorry, Mackenzie," he began and then stopped, looking at the top of my head. He smirked. "What the heck's going on with your hair?"

"I'm trying a new look. But never mind my hair. What are you sorry about?"

Kyle looked out over the pond and continued, "I'm sorry, but this isn't going to work out, this thing between us."

"This *thing*? What exactly *is* this thing?"

"You know. Being boyfriend and girlfriend."

This was news to me. We'd never actually declared ourselves to be a couple, never changed Facebook status to "in a relationship." And now Kyle was deciding that whatever we had was over, and Rational Me wanted to say, *Hey, no big deal. It's been fun. Stay in touch.*

Unfortunately, Anxious Me had control of my mouth in that moment, and I heard myself saying, "What? Why? I thought things were good. I mean, there was *hand-holding*, for God's sake! That meant *nothing* to you?"

Kyle looked at me without speaking for a long minute as Rational Me admonished Anxious Me, *Be cool! Be cool!*

It's confusing up there in my head sometimes. And crowded.

He finally spoke. "I'm moving to Bangladesh."

Okay, now, guys have broken up with me in the past. Usually, it's the general "There's someone else" or the totally understandable "My old girlfriend from grade school connected on Facebook, and I want to give it a shot with her." And of course, there is the irrefutable: "After that parole violation, they're sending me back to the slammer."

But Bangladesh? Seriously? I'd heard, "It's not you, it's me," but never, "It's not you, it's Bangladesh." This was a first.

Kyle continued. "There's some humanitarian work being done over there, and I just feel like it's something I have to do." Humanitarian work? I couldn't recall Kyle ever sacrificing anything for anyone, and suddenly he was going to be Mother Teresa?

Snarky Me wanted to say something, well, snarky, but Rational Me won the toss, and I forced myself to say, "Wow. Okay. Wow. Well then, good luck." I bit back, *Jerk!*

I could have asked him for more details about stupid Bangladesh, but I didn't feel like it. Google could tell me all I needed to know later. We walked back to my car in silence, shared a little hug—my second awkward hug of the day—and went our separate ways.

In less than twenty-four hours, I'd lost my ex, my job, and now my boyfriend. And if all that wasn't bad enough, my hair was a complete and total disaster.

If Gram was right about troubles, I'd more than met my quota, and things would be looking up from here. I drove home to my apartment and checked the time to be sure it was after noon because only somebody with a drinking problem would drink before noon. It was 12:13 p.m. when I broke my sober streak of four days with the wine I had stashed in the back of the cupboard, just in case.

Today was that case.

CHAPTER FIVE

Still Monday

WOKE AT 6:30 THAT evening on my couch with a cramp in my back and a pain in my head the size of Texas. I blamed it on the fact that I had not eaten a thing for dinner—or for lunch if I didn't count the empty boxes of Good & Plenty, Milk Duds, and Mike and Ike.

Sober Me niggled, *Or it could be all the wine you guzzled.*

Before I could argue, I remembered I had forgotten to call my mother. Cell in hand, I shuffled into my kitchen and called Gram's landline.

A couple years ago, Gram's eighty-two-year-old third husband, Nathan, started getting more forgetful. "Losing it" is how Gram put it. About that time, my mother, Barbara, who is six-ty-two, decided to sell her house and move in with Gram and Nathan to help.

The Victorian where they all live is a grand house built just after the Civil War by J.C. Crawford, who had made a fortune in the lumber industry in the area and added a bundle to that fortune later, supplying goods to the Union Army. The Crawford House would have qualified as an official historic home if a past owner hadn't made changes to the exterior.

Gram and her second husband, Chester, purchased the house and worked hard to restore it to its original glory, as far as they were able to before Chester died suddenly ten years ago.

As Gram told the story, Chester played cribbage at the Three Rivers Senior Center every Wednesday afternoon. He met this woman, Harriet, now and forevermore referred to in our family as "The Hussy." Chester and Harriet were evidently making out in her car after playing cribbage when Chester, a large man with a bad heart, bought it. The position they were in when he died, well, let's just say it was difficult for The Hussy to extricate herself. She managed to get the attention of another senior center member passing by who called 911. Too late for Chester.

The Hussy had a heck of a time explaining it all.

Gram said she wasn't too surprised since Chester always had "a way" with the ladies. "They just threw themselves at him! A man can only resist so many times," she said.

Gram buried Chester quietly and, since he had no children or other living heirs, he left her his money and the Victorian home. Chester's money was enough for Gram to afford the house's upkeep and live without financial worries.

Two years after Chester died, Gram took a Caribbean cruise. She figured Chester owed her that vacation after the way he embarrassed her with The Hussy.

On the cruise, she met Nathan, a widower, when they both signed up for ballroom dancing lessons. Nathan lived five hours away, just outside of Chicago. They hit it off and had a long-distance relationship before they decided to get married and live in Three Rivers.

I stood in my kitchen drinking a glass of water while Gram's landline rang. Gram keeps the landline and has, so far, refused to get a cell phone.

She says, "I don't need any new-fangled gizmos. A regular phone was good enough for Thomas Edison, and it's good enough for me."

"You mean Alexander Graham Bell," my mother tells her. "He invented the telephone."

"Well, I'm sure Thomas Edison had one too!" Gram huffs.

Besides her landline, Gram had, until a couple years ago, an actual answering machine. My mother convinced her to upgrade to a cordless phone with voicemail. Gram said, "Don't that beat all? It's got a built-in answering machine. I just have to dial this number and they give me my messages." I didn't bother to explain that it's all computerized, in the cloud, and "they" don't exist. After an eternity, I heard my mother's greeting: "Hi, you've reached Barbara, Virginia, and Nathan. Leave a message and have a great day."

After the beep, I said, "Call me when you have a minute, Mom. I have news. I'm fine, so don't worry." I texted the same message to my mother's cell.

Leaving my mom voicemail or texting her requires skill. The message has to be just right. Too little information, and she might not call back. Too much, and you send her into a tailspin of worry.

After leaving the message, I looked at the two empty wine bottles on the kitchen counter, thinking, *Wait. Where did that second bottle come from?* I didn't recall that I even owned a second bottle, much less that I had consumed it.

Sober Me suggested that I might want to give Dr. Angela a call.

Dr. Angela Danforth is a psychologist in private practice. She runs a clinic called Mind Over Matter, and I'd worked there briefly as her receptionist while Billy and I were married. "Briefly" was actually three weeks, until the night a client pulled a knife on Dr. Angela and me as we walked out to our cars. After that incident, Billy the Cop suggested I start carrying a gun or quit the job. I chose the latter. Guns give me the heebie-jeebies.

My mother took that job after I left, which seemed so unlike her after what happened in the parking lot. She was uncharacteristically nonchalant about it.

"Oh, pish-tush. That was just one client, one time. This is Three Rivers, not The City." She put on a brave face, but she also adjusted her working hours so she could be done before dark. And she took a self-defense class at the YMCA with my grandmother. And bought pepper spray. *Pish-tush, indeed.*

That was all well and good for my mother—until a male client decided she should marry him. He stalked her until she got a restraining order, and he moved out of state. After that, my mother quit working at the clinic and got a part-time job at Lumber City Bank. "No crazies there," she said.

Except for one, Snarky whispered.

Anyway, Angela had helped me in the past with what she called my "adjustment issues," adjusting as I was to the divorce. I liked that. I could adjust anytime without being a crazy person.

Maybe I needed some help with these new adjustments. Not now though. I had to get my life together, get to the funeral, find a job. I'd call Dr. Angela later. Maybe.

I took a couple of Excedrin and jumped into the shower. I let the hottest water I could handle run down the back of my neck, crying for a while about stupid Billy, then about losing my job and stupid Trip, and stupid Kyle moving to stupid

Bangladesh, and then getting furious for a while, yelling at Billy and Trip and Kyle.

"Stupid men! Always letting me down! I'm done with all of you!" I yelled loud enough that my upstairs neighbor, Mrs. Litowsky, pounded on her floor with her cane. She's in her seventies, and the cane is a memento of some trauma that she's never talked about in the time we've shared the building. And I don't know how to ask politely, so the secret remains.

When I first moved in, I offered to switch apartments with her, but she insisted, her German roots showing, "No, ze stairs do me goot! Besides, nobody can break in at night."

Maybe I looked worried about my first-floor vulnerability because she gave me a reassuring pat on the arm. "Not that that could efer happen here!"

Three Rivers doesn't have much crime, but as my mom says, "You never know."

I yelled at the ceiling. "Sorry, Mrs. Litowsky!" She tapped a couple more times to let me know she heard me.

This is how it is living in an old building like ours. The upside is the rent is cheap. The downside is the walls are paper-thin, and the ceilings aren't much thicker. I'm surprised Mrs. Litowsky hasn't fallen down into my place.

I calmed down as I shampooed, lathering-rinsing-repeating four times in hopes of taming the squirrel. After the shower, my Texas-sized headache had shrunk to the size of Montana. I dried off and slipped on my favorite jeans, a long-sleeved tee, and a sweatshirt. The apartment felt chilly after the heat of the shower.

My cell sounded the ringtone I had assigned to my mother. An annoying nasal voice commands, "This is your MUTH-UH! Pick up! PICK UP! WHAT'S WRONG? WHY AREN'T YOU PICKING UP?"

The only thing missing is "you must be dead in the ditch!" This is the universal fear of every mother living here in cold country during the winter driving season. "Drive carefully, or you'll end up dead in the ditch somewhere!" Way to plant the seed, mothers.

I answered and started to say, "Hey, Mom—" but she interrupted, rapid-fire.

"Mackenzie? What's wrong? You said you had bad news? What is it? Are you all right? What's going on? I've been going crazy since I got your text! Are you hurt? Are you sick?"

My mother denies that she has anxiety. She insists she is just "high strung," but we five kids learned early not to argue with our mother when she's "worked up." And she was getting worked up now, assuming that any news I had must be bad news.

I jumped in. "Mom! I'm fine. Just breathe." I listened as she took several quavering breaths, and she was calmer when she spoke next.

"Okay, Mackenzie, what's going on?"

I told her about Billy being dead.

"Oh dear. That's too bad," she said. "But I'm not surprised. That boy was always trouble. I could never understand why you would settle for someone like that. You deserved so much better . . ." Ah, her ongoing lament.

"Whatever, Mom. It's kind of too late for that now, isn't it?" She had questions. I had zero information other than Stella's opinion that he had not overdosed. I told her when the funeral was planned.

"Your grandmother won't be able to go with you. Nathan has a bunch of doctor appointments tomorrow."

"It's okay, Mom. I'll manage on my own."

"I can take the day off work if you want," she said but added that since she didn't have any vacation or sick days, she'd have to take the day without pay. "But I will if you want me to."

Hmm. My anxious mother with me on a road trip? No thanks. "It's okay, Mom. I can manage. And I have more news." I recounted the scene with Trip.

She said, "Well, honestly, Mackenzie, I always thought you were overqualified for that job. I mean, seriously, you have a bachelor's degree, for heaven's sake. You should be doing something more than being some rich man's flunky!" Again with the lament. *Arggh!*

I told her about Kyle, and she didn't disappoint. "Good riddance! And seriously? Bangladesh? The guy who spends a fortune on a bicycle now suddenly cares about poor people?"

My mother had told me a couple months ago that I "deserved better" when Kyle dropped almost three grand on his new bicycle. I had trouble defending him. Especially when Kyle insisted that we always split the check when we went out. Always. And I did the driving on dates. Always. And he never offered to help pay for gas. Never.

I repeated. "Yup. Bangladesh. Humanitarian work. That's what he said. The guy's an enigma." My mother had another word for him, which I'd thought but didn't say out loud.

"Well, thank goodness," she continued. "I expected a lot worse."

"Mom! How can it be worse? Billy's dead! I got dumped! I got fired! No income! I'll be homeless! I'll starrrrve." I stretched out that last word so she'd get the point. Her kids being anxious sometimes sent her into reassuring-mama mode.

It worked. Her voice was softer as she said, "Well, dear, you've faced challenges before. I'm sure you'll figure this out too." This was a little tip she told me she'd learned from working with Dr. Angela, to not try to solve your kids' problems but express your confidence in their ability to figure stuff out for themselves.

"I'm sure I will too. I just wanted you to know."

"Okay, honey. Let me know if I can help—" I heard a loud crash on her end of the conversation. My mother yelled, "Oh my God! What was THAT?" to Gram, most likely. This was followed by a clunk, which I guessed was my mother dropping her cell on the counter without hanging up.

"Mom, hang up! Mother! MUTH-UH!" I yelled. "HANG UP YOUR PHONE!" I could hear my mother and Gram shouting at each other in the background, the latest household calamity, no doubt. I disconnected.

As the saying goes, "Not my monkey, not my circus." I had monkeys of my own to worry about.

CHAPTER SIX

Tuesday, October 23

LEFT THREE RIVERS AT nine o'clock Tuesday morning, heading north in Charlotte the Chevy. (Yes. We name our cars.) I'd dressed in my best funeral outfit—gray cotton long-sleeved tee with a black blazer, black dress slacks, and black flats. I'm not a high-heels kind of gal.

I inherited Charlotte from my older sister, Stephanie, after she graduated college. She's an ugly green, and her chassis is rusting—Charlotte, not Steph, just to be clear—but she runs fine for an old girl with almost 200,000 miles on her.

In Charlotte's back seat, I had my "bug-out bag," aka "BOB." (Yes. I named my suitcase too.) My anxious mother taught me to always have a small suitcase packed with essentials. Bob holds undies, socks, sneakers, extra clothing, pajamas, makeup, reading material, pens, notebook, extra phone charger, battery pack for charging, snacks, water, a knife, fork and spoon, instant coffee, mug, paper plates, paper cups, can opener, antacid tablets, anti-gas pills, soap, shampoo, deodorant, tissues, toothbrush and toothpaste, and an extension cord.

Like I said, essentials. Anything you might need in case you are stranded on an island somewhere without a Target because, as Mom says, "You never know."

I also have a bag of tools (screwdrivers, wrenches, a hammer, and duct tape) on the floor behind the driver's seat. It's been there for years, and I've never used any of it. But I keep it there because, well, you never know.

I hear her voice. "You could end up in the ditch somewhere." *Yeah, Mom. The screwdriver and duct tape will come in very handy then.*

I checked the rearview mirror. My hair, after multiple shampoos, had toned down to gray-brown stripes—slightly less angry squirrel and more tired, old squirrel. My mood matched.

I was somber as somber could be, thinking about Billy and the idea I'd never see him again. We hadn't had much contact since the divorce, but even though you don't talk to someone, there's comfort in knowing they are somewhere in the world, and you could talk to them if you wanted to. Or needed to. And regardless of how everything between us ended, it had started pretty great and had been pretty great for a while.

I'd known Billy since I was sixteen. Almost twenty years. Over half my life.

In his honor, for the drive, I'd downloaded a special playlist of all the old songs we liked back then. Cruising up the highway, I cried off and on with all the young love and hopes and dreams playing into my Bluetooth. (Hands-free is the only way to drive if you don't want to end up dead in the ditch somewhere. Mama said.)

I listened to Jamma Boyz' school day classics like "Meet Me in the Stairwell" and "Detention's Not the Same Without You, Babe." We used to rock out to songs from the band Dead

Forever, who sang, "You're the One and So Am I," and "Don't Leave Me to Clean This Up Alone." Maybe not the best songs in the world, but they were ours.

The one Billy claimed as "our" song was "I'll Never Find Another," extolling the virtues of a partner who could "put up with all my stuff and never get enough." If Codependents Anonymous had a theme song, this would be it. Maybe I needed to find a group.

I stopped for gas halfway to Deerwood, checked my phone, and saw a text from Kyle. An apology? An expression of regret for ending things so suddenly? A profession of love and commitment, along with a plea for forgiveness and another chance? Nope, nope, and nope.

"U stl hv my blu swtshrt?" Kyle had an aversion to texting any more vowels than he deemed absolutely necessary, which made me glad he delivered "M gng 2 Bngldsh" in person. *That wd hv bn tuff 2 figr out,* I thought and smiled a silent LOL.

Back to the text. Translation? Ah. Sweatshirt. Blue sweatshirt. Yup. I still had the evidence of Kyle's presence in my life: the "blu swtshrt" and some socks that got soaked one day when we were out hiking. And three bottles of dark beer he left in my fridge.

Kyle fancied himself a connoisseur of dark beer. I can't stand the stuff. That's another reason, besides never drinking before noon, that I know I'm not an alcoholic. Alcoholics will drink anything, including rubbing alcohol. I have limits—no dark beer for me—so I know I'm okay.

I spent a fraction of a second wondering why Kyle would need a sweatshirt in Bangladesh. Wasn't it kind of hot there? I'd have to Google that later. Not that I cared.

I filled the tank, bought a couple of gas station donuts, and got back in the car. Kyle could darn well wait until I got back home. Right now, I was on my way to say goodbye to Billy. I could only handle one relationship closure at a time.

CHAPTER SEVEN

DEERWOOD: POPULATION 1,000 IN the winter, 10,000 in the summer. Memories: a gazillion. With woods and wildlife, lakes, and streams galore, the area is dotted with hundreds of lake homes owned by "city people" from Chicago and Minneapolis and all the places in between.

I parked behind the Bigelow Family Funeral Home, and as I walked inside, I checked the time. I was a minute early at 10:59 a.m.

The place smelled like every other funeral home—the heavy scent of all the flowers mingling with all the cologne worn by all the mourners over all the years, and another unidentifiable smell. Or maybe we know what that smell is and just don't want to name it.

I signed my name in the little book by the front door and looked around at the crowd, recognizing nobody. A thin woman, late sixties, in an expensive-looking gray dress, waved and smiled, then walked to me.

"Mackenzie? Remember me? Aunt Lois?" Oh yeah. Billy's father's sister. She extended a manicured hand, and I shook it. I said it was nice to see her again, though I had only a vague sense of having met her before, most likely at our wedding. But I may or may not have had a little too much wine on that occasion.

I asked Lois where I might find Stella. She pointed me toward the next room. I stepped through the doorway and saw him.

Billy. Casket. My throat tightened. I bit down on my tongue to keep from crying, a little trick Gram had taught me.

Stella stood with a small group of people in the middle of the room, beautiful in her dark gray suit tailored to fit her slim form, fabulous pearls around her neck, and silvery gray hair shining in the overhead lights. Perfect Stella. I waited until the group disbanded and then stepped quickly toward her, my back to the coffin.

She saw me and smiled that sad smile of the bereaved, lips pressed together, and her head tilted to the right a little bit. I tilted and smiled back.

"Mackenzie. Dear. Thank you for being here. William would be glad you came." I nodded. Today, Stella could call him whatever she wanted. She wrapped her arms around me, and I swallowed hard, willing myself not to cry. She held on to me. I finally mumbled something into her shoulder about being "so sorry" and "such a sad day," and she released me. I dug a tissue out of my purse and blew my nose.

Stella waved Billy's father, Jim, over from the other side of the room. Looking older, he was still handsome, trim, and athletic. Billy resembled his mother more than his father. Other than the occasional run, Billy preferred to watch sports rather than participate. He stayed in good enough shape to meet police department requirements, barely. And if anyone teased him about his paunch, he'd laugh and say, "Hey, I've worked hard on this belly! You know how many beers I've had to drink for this?"

Jim thanked me for coming, gave me a quick hug, and walked off to greet others. Stella put her hand on the small of my back and asked, "Do you want to see him?" Meaning Billy. Dead Billy.

Did I want to? No. Did I have to? Yes.

I nodded, turned, and she steered me forward. She patted my back. "Take your time, dear," she said and turned away.

There he was, lying there, not looking at all like Billy. I hate it at funerals when people say of the departed, "He looks so good!" Or the completely ridiculous, "Doesn't she look just like herself!" I suppose some people find this comforting. I am not one of them.

Billy looked nothing like himself. Dead is not alive. He looked empty and cold despite the makeup. *Makeup. Oh boy, what Billy would have to say about wearing makeup.* If he could have, he'd have sat up and sworn. "Somebody get this --- stuff off me!"

I felt the urge to touch his hand, but I knew it would feel as cold and empty as he looked. I smiled at him and whispered, "We had some good times, didn't we? Goodbye, my . . ." I hesitated. What fit us now? Old friend? Ex?

I leaned down close to his ear. "Goodbye, my first love."

I stood up and turned away, swallowing hard and squeezing my eyes shut against the tears. I thought a prayer for Billy, just in case there was a place somewhere up there where the final decision about where you ended up was made, which there probably wasn't. I wanted to put in a good word, just in case that counted for anything. Which it probably didn't since I pretty much stopped praying at age ten when my grandfather died and my father left. But I prayed anyway. Just in case the "higher power" or whatever was out there might be surprised enough to hear from me to give Billy a break.

I was heading toward the folding chairs in the back row of the room when I noticed a guy about my age, tall, maybe six-two, clean-shaven with a buzz cut. I can spot a cop, even when they're out of uniform, like this guy in his dark blue dockers and gray sweater stretched taut over massive biceps and impressive pecs. Not that I notice such things.

He was talking with Billy's dad, who pointed in my direction.

Cop-guy reached me and extended his hand. "Ben Marks, Deerwood PD." Ah. My Spidey-sense still worked.

He pulled a little notebook from his shirt pocket. "So, you were married to the deceased?" he said with a flat, clinical tone. Like he was asking, "You own the green Chevy in the parking lot?"

I felt a flush of anger. *The deceased?* I hate it when people in official capacities ignore the humanity of others. Like when Gram was in the hospital, and the doctor brought in a bunch of interns and referred to her, saying, "Here we have a female, elderly, presenting with—"

I'd interrupted and said, "Her name is Virginia, and she's a wife, mother and grandmother, and a person!" The doctor had stammered an apology.

I scowled at Ben. "Married to *Billy*, you mean?"

Ben's cheeks colored. "Sorry. Yes. Mr. Stone. William Stone, er, Billy."

"Yes, I was, but we're divorced."

"Sorry again. Do you think he wanted to . . . that he was . . ." Ben fumbled for the right word.

"Suicidal? Do I think he was suicidal? How the hell would I know?" I was getting sick of this guy. "And seriously? Do you think this is the best place for this conversation?" My cheeks felt hot.

"I'm sorry. You're right. Not the best time." He pulled a business card from the back of the notebook. "Please give me a call tomorrow? I'd like to get this finalized."

"Sure. Whatever."

"Sorry for your loss," he mumbled as I turned my back.

What an idiot, Snarky Me said. No part of me disagreed.

I was totally comfy in the back row, wondering what about Billy's death was left to "finalize," when Aunt Lois came and told me Stella insisted that I join the family up front. Bummer. The people-watching is so much better from the back row. And nobody can see you cry.

I sat next to Stella as the funeral proceeded. Words of comfort from a minister—the program said he was Pastor Lloyd Hanson from Jim and Stella's church. He explained that the funeral would have been at the church, but the building had been invaded by wasps and was currently being fumigated. *Bad timing, Billy.*

Pastor Lloyd read the summary of Billy's life. How is it that we can be summed up in two little paragraphs? Billy: born in Deerwood, graduated from Three Rivers High, associate degree in criminal justice from Wolf Valley Technical College. Liked to hunt and fish. Loving son to Jim and Stella, nephew of several aunts and uncles. He would be missed by family and friends. No mention of me, just one of his "friends" now.

The service wound down with all of us singing "Amazing Grace," which is pretty much a Protestant funeral staple. As we stood to sing, Stella grabbed my hand and squeezed it. I looked at her. She gave me a sad smile, tears brimming. I felt a wave of compassion for this woman, this mother, who had just lost her only child. I imagined how Gram or my mother would feel if that happened to one of us. I squeezed Stella's hand and mirrored the sad smile.

She released my hand and leaned into her husband as the casket was carried out. No burial. Cremation. I didn't want to think about that.

Billy was gone. It was over.

All over except for the lunch. I don't know if this is a universal tradition, but the "funeral lunch" is certainly a requirement around here.

It was at the funeral lunch that things got weird.

CHAPTER EIGHT

W E GATHERED AROUND THE corner from Bigelow's at a place called Slim's Tap, a bar in Deerwood that once was owned by someone named Slim. Billy and I had been frequent customers on visits to Deerwood, and Billy seemed to know everybody in the place.

Billy had told me that Slim wasn't slim at all but weighed over 300 pounds. In another piece of local irony, Slim sold the bar to a guy called Lumpy, who was not, you may have guessed, the least bit lumpy but actually slim. Lumpy's went bust, and the place was now in the hands of a local real estate guy who changed the name back to Slim's Tap, adding "N Food" to the name.

A big sign in the front window announced: SLIM'S TAP N FOOD NOW SERVING BREAKFAST AND LUNCH.

Walking in, I saw that the owner had expanded from the bar into the space next door and remodeled the kitchen, visible through the kind of serving window you see in old-fashioned diners. In the old days, there'd have been a guy named Cookie back there wearing a tee shirt with the sleeves rolled up to reveal his tattooed biceps, hollering, "Order up!" Gram used expressions like that when she cooked, harkening back to her younger waitressing days.

A sign above the archway between the old and new spaces said Banquet Room, and that's where the crowd headed. I queued up behind Aunt Lois in the buffet line.

"Isn't this a nice spread?" she said over her shoulder. I murmured agreement as I scooped potato salad onto my plastic plate. I had just started assembling a sandwich—a white bread bun I smeared with a gob of Miracle Whip, onto which I piled sliced ham—when someone tapped me on the shoulder.

I turned to see a guy about my height with a weathered face, a scruffy beard, and a couple of missing teeth. He didn't look good or smell that great either, and he looked excruciatingly uncomfortable.

"You Mack?" he said. I nodded.

He continued, "I gotta talk to you. It's real important. Meet me out back?"

I hesitated. I don't like postponing food under any circumstances, but especially when I'd only had the gas station donuts on the drive up.

"Can you give me a few minutes to eat?" I asked. He nodded and shambled off toward Slim's back door.

I turned to find a place to sit. Aunt Lois waved me over, pointing at the empty folding chair next to her. I took it, and she introduced me to the others at the table. "Of course, you remember . . ." cousin so-and-so and uncle whosit. I didn't recall meeting any of them, but I nodded with a smile as if we were old buddies.

When Lois told them, "And you all remember Mackenzie." I got a few raised eyebrows and some knowing nods. Knowing what, I couldn't be sure. How had Stella portrayed me to the extended family? Probably not as the long-suffering wife who'd put up with about as much nonsense from her cheating husband as anyone could expect. More likely, I'd been described as a conniving thief who broke poor innocent William's heart. Whatever.

Small talk out of the way, I dug into the food on my plate, typical funeral fare in these parts—hearty but bland. Gram likes to joke that the only spices we use around here are salt and pepper, and we don't like to get carried away with either. All the food on my plate was in the white to beige color palette except for the strawberry Jell-O. And even that red was muted to pink after the maker mixed in the Cool Whip.

I gobbled my lunch in less than five minutes and excused myself from the family, saying, "Nice to see you all" (thereby avoiding that awkward moment when you say "Nice meeting you" to someone you've already met but just don't remember). I slid my purse onto my shoulder, tossed my plate, plastic fork, and the Styrofoam cup holding the last sips of some very bad coffee into the trash, and stepped out the back door of Slim's Tap N Food into the warm, dry afternoon.

The months of drought had affected the entire state, especially up here in what's called "the Northwoods." The state Department of Natural Resources continued its strict ban on campfires. As Smokey Bear warned us all for decades, "Only YOU can prevent forest fires." Along the state highways, Smokey's visage still appeared on signs reading FIRE DANGER: HIGH.

There's been a lot of discussion in the last few years about the Smokey Bear effect. The message that all fire is bad has caused some forested areas to be even more vulnerable to mass destruction due to unchecked undergrowth and dead trees. Maybe ol' Smokey was too good at his job.

Regardless, a spark could ignite the woods and burn away decades of forest growth in a heartbeat when things were this dry. I certainly didn't want to be anywhere nearby when that happened.

I caught a whiff of cigarette smoke. The bearded guy sat smoking on a low concrete-block retaining wall between Slim's back parking lot and the place next door. He stood when he saw me and ground his cigarette into the dirt with his right heel. He came to me and extended a callused, grubby hand. I hesitated, then shook it.

Out here in the daylight, he looked older, in his fifties, maybe. His face carried a history of years of self-neglect. And he had sad eyes. Very sad eyes.

"I'm Walter. I was Billy's best friend. We've been tight since he moved up here, like a couple years ago, right?"

I nodded. "Nice to meet you, Walter." Billy and I had talked a couple times after we split. He'd never mentioned any friends, but we didn't exactly share details of our personal lives.

Walter continued, "I'm pretty sure someone offed him. He wasn't sick, right? He wasn't doing drugs, right?" I nodded again but realized Walter wasn't asking for my agreement. He just had an annoying habit of inserting the word *right* into his statements. Like someone injecting "you know?" repeatedly as they explain something.

Walter went on. "Somebody wanted him dead. I don't know who, but somebody . . . oh, man, somebody decided to take him out, right?" He shivered and started twitching as if he had bugs crawling under his shirt. "And now I'm worried, like maybe they'll think I knew something and they're going to take me out, too!" He glanced left, then right, and shivered again.

His fear was contagious. I looked around too. Then I shook off the feeling. Walter either had mental issues or a drug problem. Maybe both.

"Okay, Walter. Calm down. Tell me. What *was* Billy doing that someone would want to take him out?" I added air quotes.

Walter shifted and looked around again, leaned in, and lowered his voice. "I don't know for sure, but he knew something, right? And I heard him on his phone talking about having something on somebody—"

He stopped abruptly, straightened up, and shouted—I guess in case "somebody" was listening—"But he never told me nothin', and that's all I know, I swear!" He paused and then leaned toward me, confidential again. "Billy talked about you a lot, about how smart you were and how you figured things out all the time, right? Maybe you could figure this out too."

Nice of Billy to be so complimentary. I *was* pretty good at figuring things out. When we were together, I figured out the budget, the best deals on car insurance, and everything else we needed to do. But this was something else. Suspicious death is a *police* matter, not for ordinary people to try to figure out, despite what you see on television.

Walter looked like he was about to throw up, and his fidgeting got worse, head and shoulders twitching as he glanced left and right. "So, what do you think? Did somebody off him?"

"Gosh, Walter, despite this overwhelming evidence you've offered, I'm not sure."

He looked at me, hands shaking as his voice went up an octave. "What evidence?" Sarcasm was lost on Walter.

"Geez, Walter, relax. I was kidding," I said. "Have you told the police about your suspicions?"

He snorted a laugh. "You're kiddin', right? These hicks up here don't know nothin'. A bunch of . . ." He went on about Deerwood's finest, one of whom I'd already met. And although Ben Marks didn't have the sensitivity of a toad, I still don't like people disrespecting officers of the law. They are, after all, the only thing standing between us and anarchy.

I interrupted him mid-rant. "Okay, okay. I can do a little checking, ask some questions, maybe see what I can find out." I asked Walter for the names of any other friends of Billy's he thought I should talk to.

Rational Me affirmed this. *Yes, gather information. That's where the TV detectives always start.*

But Anxious Me chimed in immediately with, *What the heck do you think you're doing? This is a* police *thing! Let* them *figure it out!* I ignored her and focused on what Walter was saying, taking notes on my phone.

"There's Joe Chastain. And Andy Sanders," he said, then scrunched up his face, thinking hard. "Oh yeah. There's Box."

"Box? Is that a person?"

"Yeah, but everyone just calls him Box. Not sure why."

Walter didn't have a phone, so couldn't supply me with any numbers. I wrote my cell on a gum wrapper I found in the bottom of my purse. "Will you call me if you think of anything else that might help?" He said he'd find a phone if he needed to.

Walter looked at me. I read pain on his face—and sadness. He said, "You think someone offed him, too, right?" He swiped at his eyes with a grubby palm.

I felt a pang of pity for the guy. "Not sure, Walter, but I'll try to find out. Stay in touch." He gave me a nod and, as he shuffled off down the alley, I went back into Slim's.

The funeral crowd had thinned considerably. I spotted Stella at one of the tables and made my way over to say goodbye.

"Oh dear, do you have to rush off? I hoped we could talk a bit back at the house. The family will be heading over, and there are those things of William's, those things he left—" She took a breath and looked at me. "Stop by the house? Please?"

It's hard to resist a request from a grieving mother and maybe a mortal sin to lie to one. But I told her a big fat fib about Gram needing me back home. I told her I'd call her later to arrange a time to come back, then headed to my car around the corner in the funeral home parking lot.

I had just opened the car door when a deep voice called, "Wait up!" A big guy in camo jacket and pants, with shoulder-length black hair bouncing, trotted in my direction. I put my car keys in defense position, in a fist, with two keys sticking out between my fingers. I had seen this in a movie, I think. Or maybe it was something Gram taught me after she and my mother took that self-defense class at the Y. Keys in hand, I felt ready for an attack in case this guy got any funny ideas.

"You're Mackenzie, aren't you?" Attackers don't usually call you by name, do they? He smiled. His teeth were very straight and very white. Not likely an attacker would have such a great smile. Completely illogical, I know, but I relaxed my grip on the keys.

"Do I know you?"

Another smile. "I've seen your picture at Billy's. He talked about you all the time. I'm Joe Chastain, Billy's best friend." Now I was confused because Walter said *he* was Billy's best friend.

Joe dug into his jacket pocket and pulled out a small key. He held it toward me. "Billy said if anything ever happened to him, I was supposed to give you this. It's a key for something at the cabin, and he said it was important for you to get it. So here." As I took the key, Joe looked up at the sky and spoke aloud. "There, my friend. I did what I promised, okay? We're square now."

Joe was talking to Billy, and I didn't interrupt. I looked at the key. It was just an inch or so long, brassy, with a hole in the end. It looked like the mailbox key we had at one of our apartments. Maybe it opened a post office box somewhere.

I looked up. "Joe, do you know what the key is for?"

"Nope. Just that it's something at the cabin, and Billy said I should give it to you. That's all I know."

"When did he give it to you?"

He shrugged. "I don't know. A couple days before—" He cleared his throat and tried again. "You know, before he . . . you know."

"Died?"

Joe looked down at the ground. "Yeah. Before he died," he said softly, then looked at me. "So there. I kept my promise. Now I gotta go." He trotted off in the direction he'd come from.

I leaned against Charlotte, thinking. Billy evidently had two "best" friends who cared enough about him to come here today and talk to me. Something was going on here, and since Billy was so confident I'd be able to figure out what it was, and since I had no job and no boyfriend to get back to, I decided to stay in Deerwood overnight. Maybe I'd track down these other guys—Box and Andy—and see if they knew anything. Maybe I could check out the cabin, possibly find whatever this key would open, and see what Stella wanted to show me. And I'd told Ben that I'd give him a call. Maybe I'd make it in person.

I called my mother's cell and left a voicemail, told her I'd be home in a day or maybe two. She had a key for my place, so I asked her to check in on Tweet and Chirp. Then I drove to

Deerwood Drugs, a store that claims to have everything you need for your home-away-from-home cabin living.

I needed some food. I grabbed two beef sticks and tossed them into my plastic shopping basket along with a bag of pistachios, a box of Good & Plenty, and a box of Nips caramels. I love Nips, and eating Nips was a Deerwood must for Billy and me. I also grabbed a six-pack of Diet Coke and some sugarless gum. I don't want to rot my teeth after all.

I spotted a Dell Crossword Puzzles book of logic problems and tossed that into my basket as well. Gram loves her crosswords; she and Nathan do the daily newspaper crossword together. "Keeps our minds sharp," she says. My mother is a sudoku fan, and I love logic problems. Gram says, "We're a puzzling family." She's not wrong.

I grabbed a sweatshirt with I (heart) Deerwood across the chest. The heart had antlers. The shirt was on clearance for $2.99. Irresistible.

Billy's cousin Cammy was working the front register. Cammy and I are about the same age. She and her husband Bobby hung out with Billy and me when we visited Deerwood. We'd chatted for a few minutes at the funeral home, one of those rapid-fire conversations that can cover years in a few seconds:

"How've you been?"

"Can't complain. What have you been up to?"

"Same old, same old. How's your (husband-wife-partner-mother-whoever)?"

"Great. And you?"

"Great. Good seeing you."

"You too. We should keep in touch."

"Yes, we should."

We never do.

I put my little basket on the drugstore counter and said, "Hey, Cammy. I didn't know you were working here." Cammy had worked at Stone Enterprises since she graduated from high school. Billy had even joked that maybe instead of Stone and Son, the business would become Stone and Niece.

"I quit Stone a couple months ago. Just couldn't take all the drama anymore. This job is a lot less stress, and I can be home more with the boys." Cammy's boys were their two Great Danes.

I was curious to hear more about "all the drama" at Jim's business, but a line of customers had formed behind me. "I'm staying in town tonight. Maybe we can meet for breakfast tomorrow?"

"Can't. Sorry. Working tomorrow. But let's stay in touch."

"Sure, let's do that," I said, making a silent vow that yes, *for sure*, we would. I paid with my debit card and then drove to the Deerwood Super 8 and checked myself in.

CHAPTER NINE

'M ALWAYS RELIEVED WHEN the No Smoking sign on a
motel room door truly means that nobody ever smoked in
there, or at least it's been smoke-free long enough to dispel any
lingering stench. As I opened the door of room five, I knew
this was not the case. I guessed that the Deerwood Super 8 had
allowed smoking in the rooms until five minutes ago, when I
requested a non-smoking room, and someone ran down and
slapped the sign on the door. The room stunk. I made a mental
note to complain later, but I doubted anyone would care.

Everything in the spartan room—carpeting, dresser, headboard, beat-up desk, old chair—was in shades of brown to
match the cheap-looking brown paneling on the walls. I didn't
want to think how many holes might have been punched in
the walls before someone got sick of patching and put up the
paneling.

No mini fridge, no microwave. No sign of a hair dryer or
a coffee maker. Spartan indeed. I set the snacks I'd just bought

next to the TV, a monstrosity bolted to the top of the dresser. Why? Who wants to risk a hernia trying to steal one of those old things?

I opened Bob and took out my pajamas and other night-time essentials. I sat on the bed and gave it a little bounce. Not the greatest, but not the worst bed ever either.

The bathroom seemed to be clean. A paper banner stretched across the toilet seat promised it was Sanitized For Your Protection. Wow. I hadn't seen that little amenity since I was a kid.

I set my toothpaste and toothbrush on the countertop, which had an oblong burn mark on the edge. Not something you see much anymore since cigarette smoking has been banned just about everywhere. Hard to leave a mark like that when you're vaping.

I pictured some woman in the 1940s—her name would be Dorothy, but everyone would call her Dot—parking her cigarette there as she stood at the sink, doing up her face. Then she'd head over to Slim's for breakfast. She'd ask Cookie for an order of Adam and Eve on a raft. Whatever that was. I'd have to ask Gram later.

Rational Me piped up. *Hello? Earth to Mackenzie!* I gave my head a shake and washed my face. Then I patted on moisturizer, a dab of mascara, a swipe of lipstick, and a pinch to my cheeks. Pat, dab, swipe, pinch. A recipe for gorgeous. Well, maybe not gorgeous, but definitely not bad.

I drove Charlotte toward the Stones' lakefront home, stay-ing under the speed limit to take in the scenery. Memories kept me company as I passed old spots Billy and I had visited, roads we'd traveled. After several miles, I reached Stella and Jim's long driveway. I parked at the end of a string of cars. I checked my teeth for debris and ran my fingers through my hair, smoothing the squirrel as well as I could. I got out and locked Charlotte. As if anyone would steal her. Ha.

I trekked up the driveway—past a Lexus, two Audis, and a couple of Cadillac Escalades interspersed with various late-model SUVs—toward the sprawling one-story lake home Billy and I had visited many times. The lawn around the home, usually a lush green, had dried up over the summer.

The massive front door stood open. I heard the chatter of conversation, looked down, brushed lint from my slacks, adjusted my blazer, squared my shoulders, and walked in.

I paused in the two-story foyer, remembering.

Directly ahead, the great room with a vaulted ceiling offers spectacular views of sunsets over the lake through a two-story wall of west-facing windows. Sparkling clean windows. (Stella doesn't "do windows," of course. She has "people" for that kind of thing.)

The dining room and kitchen sit to the right of the great room. The kitchen is a cook's dream if you're into that kind of thing. I'm not. But in a kitchen like Stella's, I could be. Maybe.

A hallway to the left leads to a powder room and two spacious guest bedrooms, each with its own bath. At the end of the hall, the master suite features lake views and a luxurious *en suite* with a sauna. French doors open onto a private deck with a hot tub. *Oh, for a bedroom like that.* A girl can never get too much pampering.

I wondered, since his parents had this massive house with all the amenities of a five-star hotel, why Billy would prefer to live in that old cabin. But then, what thirty-something wants to live with their parents? We want to be free and independent, and that's how it should be when we're adults. On our own. Free.

Snarky Me whispered, *Yeah. You are totally free at this moment, aren't you? Guy-free. Job-free. Free indeed. Well done.* "Totally" free isn't that great. It's pretty lonely.

I surveyed the crowd, recognizing Aunt Lois and the others I'd seen at Slim's. Others I assumed were relatives or friends of Jim and Stella's, or maybe fellow members of the Deerwood Golf and Country Club. Deerwood has a small enclave of wealthy citizens. "Big fish in a small pond. Big deal," Billy had said. He had no time for small-town snobbery.

"Mackenzie!" Stella seemed genuinely glad to see me and pointed to the catered buffet. "Please help yourself. We'll talk later." She went into the kitchen.

Stella and Jim were certainly among Deerwood's movers and shakers. Jim's company, Stone Enterprises, manufactures hunting and fishing equipment and is one of the biggest employers in the region. The Stone brand means high-quality craftsmanship and durability in rods and reels and anything else a fishing enthusiast could want. And for the hunter, everything except guns.

Success runs in the Stone family. I recognized Jim's brother Eddie standing by the kitchen island, talking with Jim and another man. Eddie had a career selling medical supplies to doctors and hospitals, until the day he had a brilliant idea for improving a piece of equipment used in virtually every medical facility in the world. He patented his idea and then sold it to his former employer for several million.

As I recalled, Eddie owned a home in Chicago and another somewhere in the Caribbean. Eddie also owned the little cabin outside of Deerwood where Billy and I had stayed a few times. Where Billy died. Maybe Eddie had a sentimental attachment to the cabin; I couldn't imagine he had any real use for it.

Eddie saw me, waved, and walked toward me. Same old Eddie, with his skinny build and slicked-back black hair. Smarmy old Eddie, with the way he looks at you. Master of the *double entendre* when he's not being out-and-out perverted.

On more than one occasion, particularly when alcohol was involved, he had made a pass at me. *Blecch!* He was old enough to be my father.

Billy laughed when I'd complained about Eddie. "He's just a harmless old guy," Billy had said, "and who can blame him? You are pretty hot, babe." I smiled at the memory. Eddie must have mistaken that for encouragement.

"Mackenzie," Eddie said as he grabbed my arms and pulled me close. His breath was hot against my ear. "You look as delicious as ever." "Delicious" came out as "dee-LUSH-us" and I caught a whiff of booze. I wriggled free and pushed him away.

"Eddie, still as lecherous as ever," I said.

He laughed as he stepped back, then turned serious. "Too bad about Billy, huh? Jesus, I was going to sell that cabin. I got no use for the place, haven't been there in years. But Brother Jim asked if Billy could stay there, so I figured, what the hell. Better somebody staying there than having it vacant. Lots of break-ins around here lately. Probably druggies looking for stuff they can sell. But I shoulda sold the place. I got no use for it," he repeated, "since I got the place in the islands and, of course, the Chicago hovel." He laughed at his own joke. According to Billy, that "hovel" was a mansion on Lake Michigan.

Eddie was exceptionally chatty; booze will do that. I thought about asking him what he thought about Billy dying, but before I could ask, he leaned in and lowered his voice. "Hey, if you want to go out to the cabin, I'll be happy to take you there." He gave me a little eyebrow waggle.

The letch! I wanted to slap his face, but I said, "No thanks, Eddie. I know better than to get close to a snake."

He started to say something about having a snake to show me as I turned to walk away. He laughed again and called after me. "Your loss, Toots."

As I walked away, Eddie's second wife, Amanda, approached. She wore a curve-accentuating sapphire blue suit that made her complexion glow and her eyes sparkle. As tall as Eddie and twenty years his junior, Amanda had worked as his secretary after his first wife died in a boating accident.

Amanda was clearly spending Eddie's money in all the right places—clothes, jewelry, probably a personal trainer, and maybe even some well-aimed surgery like new boobs, a tummy tuck, and liposuction. That's what I'd do if I were married to a creep like Eddie.

I remembered them getting married in Vegas back when Billy and I were still together. Stella had been in an uproar and said the whole family was upset about this "gold-digging little tramp." I admired Amanda's moxie, getting the payoff after working for him. I'm sure his millions more than compensated for his family's harsh judgment.

"Mackenzie. It's been so long. I'm glad to see you here," she said, then tilted her head in the direction of Eddie. "Is he being annoying? You never know what he's going to do when he's had a few."

I shrugged. "Same old Eddie," I said.

Amanda sighed. "Some things never change. But he feels just awful about that wood stove in the cabin. Should have had it fixed years ago. And of course, he would have if he'd known, but hindsight is 20-20, isn't it? I feel awful too." Then she looked away and said, "Oh no!" I followed her gaze and saw Eddie talking with a young woman. Amanda gave a disgusted grunt. "She's probably not even legal." Amanda hurried off, probably to corral Eddie before he could do something criminal.

I was confused. The police said Billy died of an overdose. Walter had given me the idea that somebody was after Billy, had done him harm, maybe. But both Stella and Amanda mentioned the cabin's wood stove, as if maybe Billy's death was just an accident. We all knew the dangers of carbon monoxide here in the north.

I wanted to talk more with Amanda, but she was busy herding Eddie down the hall toward one of the guest rooms. I headed to the dining table in front of the tall windows overlooking the lake. The caterers had laid out food, and I was starving. I took one of Stella's beautiful china plates and got a little misty remembering being here for Thanksgiving and Christmas dinners.

"Try the roast beef," Aunt Lois said, coming up behind me. "It's absolutely melt-in-your-mouth." As I loaded my plate, Lois called to Stella as she came out of the kitchen. "Stella, that minister did such a lovely job with the service. Is he your usual pastor?"

Stella told Lois how Pastor Lloyd had come to Deerwood several years back and married a local widow who had two daughters. "Their mother died a year after they married, and Lloyd has been just wonderful. Raised those girls like his own. Kimmy, the older girl, is our local veterinarian. Her younger sister, Kassie, has had some trouble, but Lloyd is a saint. And now that the girls are grown, he's probably the most eligible bachelor in town." Stella gave a little laugh then and added, "Lois, since you're single, I'll be happy to fix you two up."

Lois laughed, "No thanks! I'm perfectly happy with my

two corgis." She waved a hand in the air and affected a British accent. "Like Her Majesty, the Queen!" Stella and Lois laughed.

I added chocolate cake with mile-high chocolate frosting to my plate of roast beef, then stepped quickly away from the table. I didn't want Stella to think she needed to fix *me* up with Paster Lloyd. Not my type. At. All.

I found a place to sit on one end of the white leather couch in the great room, balancing my plate on my knees. At the opposite end, I recognized Billy's great-uncle Stan, who had seemed ancient years ago. I was kind of surprised he was still alive.

Stan was engaged in an animated discussion with a younger man seated in an upholstered side chair. The topic of this discussion? Politics? Religion? No, and no.

Sports. Yes. Cowboys versus Broncos. Lions and Panthers and Bears. (Oh my!) Packers and Steelers and Saints. Football is the endless topic of discussion in these parts in the fall, and everybody has an opinion.

Everybody except me. Billy had been a Packers fan. Kyle was a Vikings fan. My friend Tansy likes the Broncos. My family members have their favorites as well. I've never understood the appeal and doubt I ever will. Maybe my disinterest was a contributing factor in Kyle's decision to move to Bangladesh.

Suddenly Uncle Stan stood up and yelled, "You're outta your mind! The Vikings haven't had a good season since the Tarkenton days!" His yelling startled me, and I jumped. My plate tipped, and my roast beef slid off onto the carpet. The cake plopped, frosting side down, on top of the meat. *Sad.* The cake was a total loss, but at least the chocolate frosting hadn't landed on Stella's perfect off-white carpeting.

Uncle Stan stormed off as I stared at the mess. The younger man knelt in front of me and started scooping the food off the floor and onto my plate.

"Sorry about that," he said. "Old Stan sure gets worked up, doesn't he?" Then he stood, took my plate to the kitchen, and returned with a fresh plate of roast beef and another piece of cake. He sat next to me, offered his hand, then withdrew it when he saw it was gunked up with frosting. As he wiped the frosting on a napkin, he smiled and said, "We haven't met. I'm Frank Logan. I work for Jim."

I smiled back. "I'm Mackenzie Prentice, Billy's ex-wife."

He smiled again. Nice smile. Straight teeth. Nice eyes. He had, from what I could see, nice everything. Tall, in good shape, chiseled jawline, a just-right nose, and very nicely dressed. "Ah. The ex-wife. The thief." His hazel eyes twinkled.

"Ah. You heard." He nodded. I felt the need to defend myself and, after checking to be sure nobody—meaning Stella—could overhear, I told him how Stella had accused me of stealing after Billy and I broke up.

Billy's parents had given us an antique clock when we got married—an ugly carved wooden thing, a foot or so tall, meant to sit on a mantel, we guessed. We didn't have a mantel. The clock was ornate with lots of detail and a figure on either side of the clock face. Were they swans? Angels? We were never quite sure.

We kept the hideous thing in a closet unless Stella and Jim were coming over. We had it in our first apartment, moved it with us to our next apartment. And the next. But somewhere between apartments three and four, the clock got lost.

"When we got divorced, Stella asked for it back. It had belonged to her grandmother, she said. We had to 'fess up that we'd lost it, which she didn't believe. She implied that I was hiding the clock somewhere in hopes it would be worth something someday."

Frank smiled again. Another twinkle in those hazel eyes. "It sounds hideous. I wouldn't blame you if you'd lost it"—he added air quotes—"on purpose. Regardless, Stella needs to get over it. Of course, if you show up with it on *Antiques Roadshow*, that will totally blow your story."

We laughed together. A delightful moment in an otherwise stressful day. I left my plate of food untouched as we made small talk about how great the house was, how dry the summer had been, how the heat was continuing into the fall—unseasonably warm, we agreed—and how the fire danger was so high, the highest in decades.

Frank told me how he'd graduated from the University of Minnesota with a degree in industrial design and had worked in Minneapolis, but he got tired of big city life. He moved to Deerwood two years ago when Jim hired him as his head designer.

I told him I'd heard that Cammy had left Stone. "Yeah. That was a surprise. I liked her."

"And how's good ol' Miss Taylor? Still running everything behind the scenes?" She'd been Jim's executive secretary for years. They say nobody is indispensable, but for Stone Enterprises, Miss Taylor came close. I hadn't seen her at the funeral. "How come she's not here today?"

"She left a few months ago. And rather abruptly. There one day and gone the next. Guess she decided to retire. She'd certainly put in her time."

"Where did she go? Someplace warm, I hope."

Frank shrugged. "I have no idea. You'd have to ask Jim. I'm sure she's been in touch with him."

"She worked there forever. I can't imagine her not having a big send-off."

"People change," Frank said. "Maybe she just got fed up. I left my previous job to move up here kind of on a whim. Just got sick of the hassle one day when I was stuck in traffic. Life is just too short to spend it sitting on the freeway inhaling exhaust fumes. I gave my notice the next morning. I never looked back."

Frank had taken charge of his life. Cammy had, too, and evidently, so had Miss Taylor. Why was I so willing to let others—Kyle, Trip, Billy, and their choices to dump me, fire me, hurt me—make me miserable?

I snapped back to the present as I heard Frank say, ". . . and my commute is just a few minutes."

I agreed that small-town living was great. As we chatted on, I found out Frank held a neutral position during football season, rooting for Packers, Vikings, or Bears whenever they played anyone else and being an equal opportunity rooter when they played one another. My kind of football fan.

I also discovered Frank was single, which he let me know subtly by saying, "By the way, I'm single. Are you?"

I let him know, just as subtly, that I was single by saying, "Yes. My boyfriend just broke up with me, and he's moving to Bangladesh."

Frank let out a long, slow whistle, shaking his head as he said, "That guy must be an idiot."

I chose to think Frank meant that Kyle was an idiot for breaking up with me, not for moving to Bangladesh.

A few minutes of chatting later, Frank looked at his watch and said, "I've got to get going. Early day tomorrow." He dug out a business card and handed it to me. "Here's my number—work and cell. Call me next time you're in Deerwood. I'd love to take you to lunch. Or dinner." He looked at my plate and smiled. "Looks like you don't eat much." I still hadn't touched my food.

"Yeah. Cheap date," I said. Anxious Me jumped on that immediately. *Date? He didn't say 'date'! Be cool!* My stomach did a flip-flop, a familiar feeling when Anxious Me is in the house.

He smiled what I was already thinking of as "that twinkly Frank smile." Can you fall in love in five minutes? Rational Me didn't think so; Lonely Me disagreed. I dug through my purse, found a pen and another gum wrapper, and wrote my cell number on it. I handed it to Frank.

He chuckled. "You could have just told me the number, and I could have put it in my phone. Or texted me."

Duh, Mackenzie. I blushed. "Yeah, but this is classier, don't you think? So now *you* can call *me* next time you're in Three Rivers, and I'll *let* you take me to lunch or dinner. Since I'm temporarily unemployed." I gave him the short version of what happened with Trip.

He frowned. "Then definitely lunch or dinner will be on me." We shook hands with a "nice to meet you," and I got a little melty when he laid his left hand over mine.

Frank went to say goodbye to Stella and Jim, and I went to the powder room. When I came out, I almost crashed into Amanda coming from the direction of the guest rooms farther down the hall.

"Oops! Sorry, Mackenzie! I was just settling Eddie down. You know he feels so awful about what happened to Billy. And in his cabin. That horrible old wood stove. I told him that thing was a death trap."

Again with the stove? I gave Amanda a puzzled look. "But don't the police think it was an overdose? That's what Stella said."

Amanda gave me a quick smile. "Well, if that's the case, Eddie's got nothing to worry about. Nice to see you again, Mackenzie. Take care." She walked away.

I started thinking. What if Billy killed himself by blocking the stove vent pipe? Do people really carbon-monoxide themselves on purpose? If he *did* want to end things, that seemed to be a relatively painless way to go. At least, that's how it looks on TV. I'd watched a lot of the Murders and Mysteries channel with Gram, where the victim is found slumped over the steering wheel in a garage full of fumes. They always look like they're just sleeping.

And here in cold country, we're reminded to have carbon monoxide detectors in the house during winter heating season, lest we die in our sleep from CO poisoning. Between CO danger and Christmas tree fires and driving on ice-covered roads and ending up "dead in the ditch somewhere," fall and winter can be hazardous to your health.

But I thought I'd heard that CO poisoning left the victim with very red coloring. Billy hadn't looked that way when I last saw him. But he had been dead then and wearing makeup, so it was hard to tell what happened before that.

And another question: Would the cabin have needed heating, given how warm it had been?

I had more questions and no answers. But I also knew I wanted to find out what really happened.

CHAPTER TEN

B Y LATE AFTERNOON, THE crowd was gone, and Stella was finally free. I decided to clear the air about the old clock and apologize one more time for the misunderstanding.

Her eyebrows shot up. "That ugly old thing? I always hated that clock, but my mother insisted on giving it to us when we got married. I think she probably hated it, too, and just wanted to get rid of it."

"We told you we lost it, but you implied you thought I stole it. I felt like you hated me for that."

"Oh, for heaven's sake, I've never hated you," she said. "I was just so upset that you and my son split up. You were good for him, and I've just been so ashamed of how he behaved. He treated you so badly." Huh. Wonders never cease. "And the clock? Good riddance!" She hugged me then, and I let her. "Come with me. The box William left for you is right in here," she said, leading me into the wood-paneled study off the kitchen.

Jim's man cave. Brass lamps came on automatically when we walked in. Floor-to-ceiling bookshelves flanked a huge fireplace, clad from the hearth to the ceiling in the most exquisite tile I'd ever seen. Decorative sailboats and fishing-related tchotchkes dotted the room around a dark leather sofa and two matching side chairs, all button-tufted and nail-head-trimmed. A dark wood coffee table and side tables completed the ensemble.

I have "stuff" in my house. Rich people have "ensembles."

Stella started to say, "Will—" then stopped. She took both my hands in hers, met my eyes. "You called him Billy. Yes, Billy."

"He's still your William," I said.

She nodded wordlessly, blinked back tears as she let go of my hands and gestured toward the cardboard box on the coffee table. "He—Billy—left this for you."

The Amazon-swooshed box was maybe twelve inches in all directions, with my name written on the top in black marker. Billy's scrawl. The box flaps were taped shut. I wondered if Stella had snooped. My mother would have. Heck, I would have too.

As if she read my mind, Stella said, "I haven't looked inside." She sat on the sofa. I settled in next to her and paused, exhaling loudly. Billy and I had pretty much divvied everything up when we split. What could he possibly have held on to?

I opened the box and pulled out a handful of DVD cases, all the old scary movies we liked. A sticky note on the top DVD case read: "Good time. Memories like a warm blanket." Ah, yes, so many nights with Billy, curled up under a blanket on the couch, eating popcorn and drinking Kool-Aid, watching *Poltergeist. Rosemary's Baby. The Shining. The Exorcist.* Classics all. I'd told Billy to keep them; I couldn't stand the thought of watching them without him.

I turned to Stella, "We used to watch these over and over when we were first married, you know, when you're first married and can't afford to go out?" She looked blank as if she and Jim had never had those lean days.

I set the DVDs aside, dug in, and pulled out a green tee shirt with Run With The Cops printed in white letters on the front. The Three Rivers PD held a race every year to raise money for charity; we'd gotten the matching shirts with our donation and ran the 5K together one year. Well, I walked after the first block or two, and Billy ran the rest of the race without me.

When I neared the end of the race, I looked ahead and saw him hugging a tall blonde. When he saw me, he let go of her and trotted over, applauding as I crossed the finish line. "Way to go, Slug!" he teased.

"Who was that?" I asked.

"Who was who?" He could fake innocence like nobody's business.

"That blonde you were hugging?"

"Oh, her? Just some random girl," he said. "She was so excited to finish, she just hugged me." I accepted that. I didn't want to think anything else. As I discovered later, that "random girl" was the very un-random girl that Billy worked with and was sleeping with at the time. I have no idea if she was the first or the tenth. Billy was busy, and I was in denial. We see what we want to see.

Coming back to the present, I looked at the race shirt. "Why didn't he just toss this?"

Stella shrugged. "Who knows?"

At the bottom of the box lay a nine-by-twelve manila envelope with my name on it. I lifted it out and removed the tape sealing the flap. I slid out a thick wad of Billy's statements from Deerwood Citizens Bank. A yellow Post-it on top read: "Mackenzie: I made you beneficiary on all my accounts. Love, Billy." I showed that to Stella.

"Interesting," is all she said, her voice a whisper.

A quick scan showed he'd used his debit card to pay for just about everything he needed. Groceries and gas, but also purchases at Slim's and the two other bars in Deerwood.

"He spent money in the bars, Stella. Don't you think that means he wasn't sober?"

Stella frowned. "But you know there isn't a lot to do in Deerwood. People like to watch sports or meet friends, and there aren't a lot of options except the bars."

I could see that.

The savings account showed regular deposits of several hundred dollars, with a larger deposit every month or so. The balance in the account as of the previous month was just shy of fifty grand. I let out a soft whistle as I handed Stella the statement.

Her eyebrows shot up. "My goodness," she said and thought for a moment. "Well, he did odd jobs for people around here, taking care of lake homes, landscaping. Handyman kinds of things. And he did some things for his father as well. I'm not sure what their arrangement was."

Billy would have needed some kind of income to support himself. But this was a lot more than he would have needed, living on the cheap in that cabin.

I slipped the bank statements back in the envelope, feeling unsteady. "Why would he do such a thing? Why leave it all to me? You're his parents, his closest family. Why me?"

Stella gave a little laugh. "Well, obviously, we don't need it! Maybe he just wanted to do something nice, to make up for how he treated you."

I looked into the box to make sure I'd gotten everything. *Any more surprises for me, Billy?* A brown paper bag lay at the bottom. I'd almost missed it since it was the same color as the box. I picked it up. I opened it.

Cash. I pulled out a wad of bills a couple inches thick. I fanned the stack. It looked to be all hundreds. "Geez Louise! There must be twenty grand here. Maybe more," I said.

"My Lord!" Stella said.

A note on lined notebook paper lay on top of the money. "Mack. This is for you. For the good times." I swallowed hard; yes, there were good times. The note continued. "I should have made my amends in person, but I want you to know you never did anything wrong. I was stupid and I'm sorry for all the pain I caused you. I hope this helps. Love you forever, Billy."

My throat tightened. This was how Billy and I signed cards to each other. "Happy Birthday . . . love you forever." "Happy Anniversary . . . love you forever." "Merry Christmas . . . love you forever."

Forever turned out to be a lot shorter than I thought.

I handed the note to Stella, and while she read silently, I lost it. I sat and sobbed while Stella rubbed my back, whispering. "I know, dear, I know."

I excused myself and went to the powder room. I splashed cold water on my face and slurped a handful of water from my palm. Staring at my reflection—eyes red and puffy—I said, "What the hell, Billy? What the hell?"

I splashed my face again, drying it on the softest hand towel in the universe, took a couple deep breaths, and went back to the study.

Stella looked at me. "William was always such a good boy, never gave us a minute's worry. Until high school, that is." Stella had never said anything negative about her darling William.

I pressed for more. "Billy never gave me any details about

what happened back then. He just said there were too many rules to suit him. What really happened?"

"He and his father got into some terrific arguments, behind closed doors, of course, but I could hear the shouting. I think it had something to do with Jim's brother Eddie, but I can't be certain. Jim just informed me one day—" Her voice broke. ". . . that he was sending our son away to live with Jim's sister in Three Rivers. Just like that." She snapped her fingers, sniffed, and wiped the tears from her face.

I felt a well of compassion. "Stella, I can't imagine how difficult that had to be for you as a mother." I had the urge to hug her, but she straightened her back, composed her face into a serene smile, and waved my comment away. Back to Stella-in-control.

"Well, yes, but I don't dwell on the past. I want to forget all that and remember William as the sweet boy he was before all his troubles." She shifted gears. "I've never really trusted Eddie, you know. Jim's tolerated him, been the good big brother, but I've never had much tolerance for his shenanigans."

Interesting word—shenanigans. Could mean anything from good-natured fun to serious criminal activity. Who knew what sleazy Eddie was doing back then? But I could imagine him involving Billy.

I didn't want to walk around Deerwood with a wad of cash. Stella offered to keep it in the wall safe, walked over to a painting of a sailboat, and pressed on the frame. The picture swung away from the wall.

"Geez, just like on TV, Stella."

"I know. This whole man cave is such a cliché, isn't it? Jim loves this gentleman's club vibe. I can't stand it. I don't spend any time in here."

71

She deftly spun the safe's lock and swung the metal door open. Before we put the cash inside, we counted it.

"Forty-eight thousand, five hundred." Stunned, I put the money back in the bag, and Stella set it in the safe. She closed the door and spun the lock again.

"There. Safe and sound." Then she giggled. "Huh. Is that where that expression comes from?" She chuckled again.

I got serious. "Stella, Billy must have planned all this, leaving me the money and making me his beneficiary. Don't you think that's a sign that he—"

She held up a hand. "Please. Don't even go there. I can't think about that."

"I talked to a couple of his friends after the funeral. They thought maybe something was wrong. Do you have any idea what might have been going on?"

"No, I don't. William wasn't one to talk about his personal issues, at least not with me. But if there was something going on, I'm sure the police will figure it out."

"Yeah, maybe." I let the subject drop.

I told her I was staying at the Deerwood Super 8, and she said, "You certainly are welcome to stay here, Mackenzie. We have plenty of room." I knew that family members were already staying with Jim and Stella, including Eddie and Amanda. I declined. I didn't want any late-night surprises from the lecher.

I told her I'd call her the next day and let her know what I decided to do about the cash. Then I gave her a hug, offered my condolences again, took the box, and went out to my car.

I sat in the driver's seat and looked at the box on the passenger's seat, thinking. *Billy! Where did you get the money? Oh my God! Almost a hundred grand! Where did you get it, and why did you give it to me?*

Okay, I might even have said those things out loud. Then I thought about Walter and Joe "talking" to Billy, so I talked to myself instead. "Geez, Mackenzie, get a grip!"

On the way back to the motel, I called my mother and told her I'd be home the next day. I didn't mention the money because that would have led to questions I didn't have answers for.

Back in my room, I dined on beef sticks and almost a whole box of Nips, washing it all down with lukewarm Diet Coke. I tried to unwind with a logic problem.

Five couples taking up five different sports, none of them playing with their spouses. Who is doing what with whom? I gave up, too tired to think. I spent the night in fitful sleep, dreaming of being lost in the big city. That's a recurring theme in my dreams—me, lost, trying to find my way home.

CHAPTER ELEVEN

Wednesday, October 24

I WOKE UP BEFORE THE sun with another headache. Maybe I needed to see a doctor. I dug through my purse and found my little metal pill box engraved with the initial *M*. Tansy had given it to me on a past birthday. I popped two Excedrin, washing them down with tap water in a plastic motel cup. The water tasted a little like dirt. Yuck. A couple rinse-and-spit maneuvers helped, but not much.

After a hot shower, I felt a little better. The headache was subsiding as I dressed in my jeans and yesterday's gray long-sleeve tee, then layered on the I (heart) Deerwood sweatshirt. I shoved my feet into my ASICS, an amazing pair of shoes my mother, the runner, had encouraged me to buy. Even though I am not a runner. And never will be, no matter how amazing the shoes are.

I locked the room, then walked down to the motel manager's office. "The water in my room tastes like dirt," I told a heavy-set woman behind the counter.

"Yeah, that's the drought," she said. "Tastes weird, but it's not harmful." She reached under the counter and produced two bottles of water. "Here ya go. No charge."

I thanked her and put the water in my room. I got in my car just as my cell chirped.

A text from Frank. "Nice to meet you yesterday. Are you free for dinner on Friday? Frank." I smiled. The man was not afraid to text a vowel. The day was improving by the minute.

I didn't want to seem too eager, so I waited until I'd parked in front of Slim's before I texted back. "Yes, Frank, I am free on Friday for dinner." (I resisted adding, *and anything else you have in mind.* Gotta play a little hard-to-get.) I texted back my address, agreed on the time, and we wished each other a good day with a couple of smiley emojis.

I smiled a real-life smile as I went into Slim's. A little bell over the door jangled my arrival. Nobody noticed me. I picked a table along the far wall and sat, looking over the menu that was propped on the table. After a few minutes, a guy with food stains on his dingy white tee shirt came out of the kitchen. He took my order with a scowl. If he'd been in a better mood, I'd have asked him if his name was Cookie.

The Deerwood Special was a hearty plate of pancakes with two eggs and bacon. I ignored the glass of murky water on the table and washed breakfast down with a decent cup of coffee that carried nary a hint of dirt.

While I ate, I worked on my logic puzzle. Anytime I'm eating alone in public, I like to have something—a book, a puzzle—so I look like I'm alone by choice, as if I'm taking a break from my busy social life and enjoying some Me Time. *Not alone because I got dumped. No. I'm popular, and I'm oh-so-very busy with all my friends and boyfriends, and heaven knows a girl just has to take a break once in a while. So, people, please do NOT talk to me while I'm enjoying this rare—very rare—time by myself.*

As if anyone notices. As if anyone cares. *Geez, Mackenzie, get over yourself.*

I was almost done eating when I heard yelling from the direction of the kitchen. I glanced toward the open space above the counter. The cranky guy was chewing somebody out for being late. A minute later, a waitress came out of the kitchen, tying on an apron as she hurried toward my table.

"Sorry about the fuss back there," she said with a jerk of her head toward the kitchen. "Anything else for you?" Her nametag said Andy, and she was pregnant. Her short black hair had purple streaks. Multiple piercings glittered from her ears, and a gold ring adorned her left nostril. I'm okay with an ear piercing, maybe a couple. But lips, noses, tongues, or other sensitive body parts? Ouch.

Her left arm sported a tattooed pattern of flowers, soft and delicate; her right arm displayed an intricately patterned snake, which circled her wrist and wound up her arm, disappearing under her shirt sleeve. Body art equals pain in my book. Double ouch.

I wondered if this was the Andy-friend-of-Billy's that Walter had mentioned, so I asked.

She frowned. "Who wants to know?"

"I'm Mackenzie. Billy and I used to be married." Andy hesitated, giving me the once-over. Then she smiled and extended a hand. I shook it.

"Nice to meet you. I'm Andy Sanders. Billy talked about you. A lot. Sorry I missed the funeral. I wasn't feeling that great yesterday. You know how it is." She patted her belly with her left hand. No, I didn't know, having never been pregnant. I noticed the lack of a wedding ring and wondered if she would be a single mom or if, as I'd heard from my sister-in-law, swollen fingers meant removing rings.

"Is it a boy or a girl?" I asked. Andy smiled, and her eyes went all dreamy.

"I'm going to let everyone be surprised." Ah. The old-school approach. Kind of rare in these days of ultrasounds and gender reveal parties, which seem at times to be just more clamoring for social media attention. But what do I know?

I shifted away from baby talk. "I met Walter and Joe yesterday," I said. "Walter had some theories about Billy's death."

"Oh, those two," Andy chuckled. "They're so paranoid. Too much you-know-what." She brought her hand to her mouth, pinching thumb and forefinger together. She sucked in her breath, then laughed again.

"Ah, yes," I said, chuckling with her. Then she got serious.

"Shame about Billy. Such a good guy. Too bad he had to die, especially like that. I'll miss him." She laid a hand on her belly again, looked down, and added, "*We'll* miss him."

I wanted to ask if she and Billy had been involved romantically and find out what she meant by him dying "like that," but several more customers had come into the café. Andy handed me my check and excused herself.

I looked down at the bill—less than five bucks for that huge breakfast. You had to love small-town living. Andy had written "Thanks!" with a smiley face. I set a ten-dollar bill on the table; a hard-working, pregnant waitress deserved a good tip. And I had, after all, just become a wealthy woman.

I turned the check over and wrote my cell number and a note saying I'd like to talk with her some more about Billy. Then I gathered my purse and my logic puzzle book and headed out to my car. Before I got in, I remembered something.

I went back into Slim's. Andy was at the cash register, ringing up my check. She saw me and smiled. "Thanks for the tip!"

I smiled back. "Yesterday, Walter mentioned that someone named Box was a friend of Billy's. Do you know how I can reach him?"

Andy frowned. "That loser? God only knows where he is."

"What kind of name is Box?"

"Short for Boxleitner," Andy said. "First name's Eric, but nobody ever calls him that. His folks live out on Highway G, just west of town. You can't miss it; there's a ton of junked cars and other crap in the yard. I think they're hoarders. They might be able to tell you where Box is."

"Thanks," I said. "And one other thing? You said something earlier about how Billy died. What did you mean?"

A flash of something crossed her face. There and gone. The smile returned. "Oh, just that he was all alone." She looked up as the little bell above the door tinkled. More customers. She picked up her order pad and pen and said, as she walked away, "So awful to be alone."

Whatever else she knew, I wasn't going to hear about it. I thanked her and left. Before heading out Highway G, I swung by the Deerwood Police Department.

CHAPTER TWELVE

I PARKED ON THE STREET in front of the Deerwood PD, which was housed in a single-story brick building around the corner and a couple blocks from Slim's. I walked into a single room with three gray metal desks crammed together and a bank of beige file cabinets lining the far wall. Two of the desks were piled a foot deep with files and papers.

A black poster on the wall had a blue line running down the center, and in white script, these words: "If this line offends you so much, you might want to stop crossing it."

Ben Marks was alone, seated at the one clean desk tapping on a laptop, wearing his dark blue police uniform. He stood when I came in. "Thanks for stopping by. I'm glad you caught me in the office."

He smiled, and I noticed how the blue of his shirt played up the blue of his eyes. *Stop it! You're mad at this guy, remember?*

He gestured toward the metal chair next to the desk. We sat. A nameplate on the desk read SGT WILLIS, next to a bobblehead of a cop with a beard. It waggled its head at me. I pointed at it. "Sergeant Willis, I presume?"

"Yeah, we all got one of those last Christmas."

I looked around, didn't see any bobblehead Bens in the room. "Where's yours?"

He shrugged. "I don't know what happened to mine." I didn't believe him; I suspected he'd probably hidden it, lest the local "perps" would think he wasn't a badass cop. *Ooh. Tough guy.*

"And where's your desk?" I asked. I had a desire to check his desk for photos of a wife and kids. *Stop!*

"This is kind of everybody's desk," he said. "We're either out on patrol or inside doing reports. Always plenty of reports."

"You have a lot of crime here? Deerwood's not exactly the big city."

Ben leaned back in his chair, crossed his arms, and gave me a half-smile. "I know your ex was with Three Rivers PD. That's not exactly Chicago either." I leaned back, crossed my arms, and smiled back.

He went on. "We get our fair share of action up here. Moving violations, drunks on the road, break-ins. Some domestics, too, in the summer from the tourists, usually when they've been partying. Locals get riled up too, but more often in the winter. You know, cabin fever? Folks get a little sick of being cooped up."

"I heard about the cabin break-ins." Eddie had mentioned them between sleazy comments.

"Yeah, several cabins, the drugstore, the vet clinic, the grocery store. All have had break-ins over the last couple months."

"Seems like a lot for a little town like this."

"It's unusual, yes, especially in the off-season. We've got some suspicions but nothing concrete." *A crime wave in little old Deerwood. Who'd a thunk it?* I wondered if any of that was connected to Billy, or to his death.

I steered the conversation back to the business at hand. "What did you want to ask me yesterday at the funeral?"

Ben reddened. "I'm sorry again about my timing. Can we just rewind the clock and pretend it never happened?"

If we could rewind time, Billy'd still be breathing. Ben seemed genuinely sorry, so I decided to cut him some slack. "Forget it."

Ben sat forward and put his fingers on the keyboard. "Your full name?"

I gave him name, address, date of birth, and phone number.

"You were married to the deceased—er, to William Stone. Is that correct?"

"Billy. Call him Billy." I gave him the dates of our marriage and divorce. I spared the details about the cheating and lying, the heartbreak of it all.

"And what do you know about his passing?"

Not a damn thing. I shook my head as I shrugged. "What do *you* know?"

"Officially, overdose," he said, tapping keys. "The autopsy . . ." I shuddered. He read from the screen. "Preliminary results indicated overdose. Final will be available in four to six weeks." He tapped again, scrolled with the mouse, read aloud. "Officers on scene found the deceased on the couch with drug paraphernalia near the body." He looked up. "I was there with Sergeant Willis at the scene. No reason to think this was anything other than an overdose."

"But what about his mother insisting Billy was sober? His friends saying the same thing? Doesn't that merit more investigation?"

"People relapse every day," Ben said. "It's unfortunate, but it happens all the time."

Angry Me didn't like his tone. "I *know* that. But with people saying he was clean and sober—"

"Relapse happens," he said. Flat. Dismissive.

I tried another angle. "Some members of his family were concerned about the wood stove in the cabin. Is it possible he died of carbon monoxide poisoning?"

Ben frowned. "No evidence of that either. He probably hadn't used the stove since it's been so—"

I finished his thought. ". . . unseasonably warm. Yes. Okay." I shifted gears again. "But another thing. His friend Walter—"

Ben interrupted me. "Ah. Walter Brown. Not the most trustworthy person around."

"Regardless, Walter seemed to think someone had something—"

Ben cut in again. "Walter has been in and out of institutions for years. He's given to delusions and some other pretty serious mental health issues, so I wouldn't put much stock in what he says."

Ben was just going to shoot down every theory, so I didn't mention Joe Chastain and the key he'd given me. I was going to have to figure things out myself.

I held up my hands. "I give up," I said, shaking my head and giving Ben my saddest sad look.

He considered me for a long moment. Then he leaned in, lowered his voice, and said, "Okay, so no *official* investigation is warranted, but if you want, I can do some checking, unofficially."

That was comforting, at least a little. "Thanks for doing that. I appreciate it."

"Well, I'm not making any promises," he said as he escorted me to the door. I was halfway out the door when I remembered something else. I turned back to Ben and asked, "Do you have any theories about what caused Miss Taylor to leave Stone Enterprises so mysteriously?"

He thought a moment. "Oh, yeah, I remember that. Nothing mysterious about it. Her sister reported her missing. We investigated. The lady left. Had every right to do that. People do what they do for reasons of their own. No evidence to indicate foul play. She took her stuff and left town. That's all."

I started to say, "But—" and Ben held up his hand. I closed my mouth.

He leaned toward me. "No. Foul. Play." He smiled again. "I will do some checking about Billy, though, just so you can have some closure."

I thanked Ben and left, then sat thinking in my car. Closure? Is that what I was seeking? Maybe. Why else would this be bugging me? Maybe it was Stella's doubts or what Amanda had said about the stove. Maybe it was Walter's worries or Joe giving me the little key.

And the big question: What caused Billy to decide he needed to get his affairs in order, make his amends, and leave me all that cash? He expected something to happen to him. And if that was the case, why didn't he go to the police? Or tell his parents? Or leave me something to explain what he was worried about? Maybe a note saying, "If you're reading this, I must be dead, and the person who killed me is . . ."

The autopsy said overdose. I couldn't see how all these other little pieces fit into the puzzle. I needed to figure that out, for Billy, for his family, for myself.

Ben was willing to do some unofficial checking, and he seemed to be competent enough. Maybe he shared some of my doubts; maybe he was asking himself some of the same questions. Walter had implied the Deerwood PD was a bunch of doofuses, but Walter no doubt had personal reasons for not liking the police.

Ben wasn't a bad sort, and he was kind of cute, all official in his blue shirt and shiny badge. Lonely Me said, *You're just a sucker for a guy in uniform.* I smiled, remembering how good Billy looked in his uniform. *He looked good out of it too,* Lonely Me reminded me as I got in my car and headed toward Highway G.

CHAPTER THIRTEEN

ANDY WAS RIGHT. THE Boxleitner place was a junkyard. As I pulled into the driveway, three dogs of uncertain parentage and various sizes—L, XL, and XXL—charged the car, barking like crazy. Their tails were wagging, but I'd read somewhere that the tail wag doesn't necessarily signal "happy to see you." In this case, I was pretty sure their wagging tails meant, "Oh goody! Here's lunch!"

I sat in the car while they barked and drooled all over Charlotte. After a couple of minutes, the biggest dog cocked its head and ran toward the house, the other two in its slobbery wake. A moment later, a man, who looked to be somewhere north of fifty, wearing grease-stained gray coveralls, came around the corner of the house and walked toward my car. No sign of the dogs, so I opened the car door and stepped out.

"Are you Mr. Boxleitner?"

He nodded and pulled a filthy cloth from his pocket, wiping his hands as he eyed Charlotte. With only slightly more metal than rust, Charlotte would have fit in nicely among his heaps of junk. "Ya lookin' to sell or buy?"

I told him who I was.

He stuck the cloth back into his pocket, and I was afraid he was going to try to shake my hand, but he shoved his hands into his back pockets and said, "Damn shame about Stone. Damn shame."

I murmured agreement and then told him I was looking for Eric.

His face clouded. "What ya want him for?"

"I was told he was a friend of Billy's, and I'm just trying to . . ." I heard Ben in my head. ". . . to get some closure. You know, so I can understand what happened?"

His mouth twisted in derision. "What do you mean *what happened*? He died. *That's* what happened."

"Of course, but some people are saying maybe it wasn't what it seems to be," I said, "and I'm just trying to get as much information as I can. You know, to understand why he died."

He took a half-step back. "You a cop?" I shook my head. He fixed me with a look, gave a snort, and said, "Well, I got nothin' to tell you. He died. End of story. There's your damn closure." He snorted again and got louder. "And Eric didn't have nothin' to do with that mess over there. Nothin'! Now, unless you want to buy something, we're done here."

He turned to walk away, but I gave it one more shot. "I don't suppose you could give Eric my number, just in case he wants to talk to me?"

He glared back at me. Even though I'm not the sharpest tool in the shed, I could tell the answer was no. I held my palms toward him in surrender. He stomped away, shaking his head.

I called after him, "Okay, then. Thanks so much. I'll be going now." He shot me the finger over his right shoulder.

I got in my car, backed out of the driveway without (I'm only a little ashamed to admit) even looking to make sure a dog wasn't in the way, and headed back toward Deerwood.

A mile or so down the highway, I pulled to the shoulder. I called Stella but got her voicemail. I'd try later. Meanwhile, I decided to drive out to the cabin, just in case it was open and I could take a look around.

CHAPTER FOURTEEN

I PULLED THE OLD-SCHOOL PAPER map from Charlotte's glove compartment. (Thanks, Mom, for teaching us kids to carry and decipher such maps because, well, "you never know if GPS is accurate.") I traced the maze of country roads and county highways with my finger and found Darby Lake. Highway M to County Road P. That should take me to Maxwell's Store, as I recalled. A final turn there onto the road to the cabin.

The October sun shone brightly over parched cornfields and desiccated meadows against a backdrop of distant trees. The long drought had made the autumn leaf display even more beautiful than usual over the last few weeks, with brilliant yellows, rich oranges, and deep rusty reds against the intense blue of the sky.

Hardship and pain do that, making the glorious moments even more spectacular by comparison. That's what Gram says, anyway.

Just when I thought I was lost, I rounded a curve and saw Maxwell's, or rather what was left of it. The front half of the old wooden structure had collapsed in on itself. I might not have recognized the place, but the sign near the road still stood.

MAXWELL'S. BAIT. EATS. GAS.

Billy and I had stopped at Maxwell's on our trips to the cabin to stock up on, well, bait, eats, and gas.

I turned left at Maxwell's onto Darby Lake Road, passing more shriveled cornfields and fields of dead grass and weeds. Houses were few here. After a couple of miles, I started seeing more driveways on my right, closer and closer together, access points to the cabins that crowded the lakefront property.

The last mailbox had STONE on it in reflective letters. I turned into the narrow driveway. A car came toward me with Amanda at the wheel. We pulled alongside one another, each lowering our driver's side window.

"Hi, Mackenzie. This is a surprise." Amanda had a scarf tied around her hair and dark smudges on her cheek. "I was just cleaning the cabin," she explained.

"I thought I'd come out and take a look around, for old times' sake."

"Sure. No problem. Take your time," she said and drove off.

The last cabin in the line of several, Eddie's property abutted a field of cornstalks and tall grass. Navigating the bumpy driveway, I drove slowly.

Then there it was. The cabin. And the memories. I stepped out of the car and took a deep breath of lake air.

The glassy surface of the water reflected the bluest of blue skies and the colorful trees on the far shore. A loon called, a plaintive song that brought back memories of sitting here by the water with Billy, just sitting without a word, enjoying the view, the quiet, the peace.

Billy loved it here. And I loved being here with Billy. I could feel his touch then; he'd reach out to hold my hand while we sat in the Adirondack chairs. No need for words. Just Billy and me and the water.

Billy and me, laughing on the boat. He teased me for feeling sorry for the fish we caught. "Don't think poor fishy," he said. "Think yummy dinner."

Billy and me. Sitting on the beach, campfire blazing, laughing, and talking into the night.

Billy and me in the cabin, making dinner. Making plans. Making love.

These were good memories, and I wanted to hold on to them. It was time to let the good times wipe out the hurt I'd felt when Billy did what Billy did—cheated, lied, and eventually left. And now he was gone. Forever.

Forever is forever. No chance for one more conversation to set things right. Grief comes in waves, they say. I felt an acute longing in that moment to see Billy one more time. But that was impossible. I felt empty suddenly and lost.

I took a couple of deep breaths to clear my head. The day was warm. The water level at the lake's shore was lower than I remembered, revealing several feet of sandy shore, assorted trash and dried weeds, and a slight stench of dead fish. More effects of the drought.

I walked toward the cabin. As I climbed the five steps to the front door, a critter scurried out from under the stairs and ran off into the cornfield. A chipmunk, maybe. I tried the front door. Locked.

In the past, the cabin was often left unlocked in the summer. Eddie had mentioned recent break-ins in the area, which Ben had confirmed. Amanda had locked up when she left. I guess Deerwood people had to be as careful about locking doors as city people these days. Maybe my mother was right. Maybe you can't trust anyone anymore.

I peered through the window into the cabin. A kitchen living room combination spanned the front. In the back were two bedrooms with a bathroom in between. Nothing fancy. Just cozy.

A black, cast-iron, pot-bellied stove in the main room provided the only heat for the place. The bedrooms were chilly most nights. Billy said that was a good thing because it forced us to "huddle together for warmth," which, of course, always led to other things. I smiled. Billy was always a good huddler.

I really wanted to get inside, to look around for whatever it was that fit the key Billy wanted me to have. Walking around the cabin, I saw that the bathroom window in the middle of the back wall was open just an inch or so. I thought about it. Could I climb into the cabin through this window? Should I?

I fingered the little key in my jeans pocket, listening to the argument in my head. Rational Me said, *That's breaking and entering.*

Brave—or maybe Foolish—Me answered, *Yup. But who's gonna know?*

Anxious Me warned, *No, no, no! Don't do it! We'll get arrested,* even as I used the little key to slit the window screen along the bottom edge, where the screen met its wooden frame.

I slid my finger inside, unhooked the screen, and swung it toward me, lifting it off the hooks that held it in place at the top. As I leaned the screen against the cabin, Anxious Me said, *Well, now you've done it!*

Brave-Foolish Me quoted Gram, *In for a penny, in for a pound.* I reached up on tiptoe and pushed the bathroom window up another inch or so. It slid up easily.

Snarky Me saw the problem immediately. *Okay, genius. How you gonna get your butt through that window?*

I'd passed a stack of firewood on my way to the front door. I made several trips, hauling pieces to the back of the cabin until

I had stacked a pile high enough to climb up on and then into the window.

People on TV make this stuff look easy. It's not. It is incredibly difficult to climb up something as unsteady as a makeshift wood pile, hoist your entire body weight over a window ledge, and then propel yourself into a bathroom. And the toilet is always right there in front of the window.

I ended up, as Gram would say, "tush over teakettle" on the floor in front of the toilet, panting from the exertion. The toilet seat was up, the bowl filthy with God-knows-what. I gagged.

Disgusting! I heard echoes from the past. *Billy! Please! Put the seat down when you're done!* I stood up, slammed the lid down, and flushed. I waited for the flush to finish and pressed the lever again. Nothing. I lifted the lid on the tank. Nothing there but rust. The water in the cabin must have been shut off, and that flush had used the last of the water in the tank.

I stood up, holding on to the edge of the sink as I let my heart slow down and my stomach settle. Amanda said she'd cleaned. *Oops, Amanda, you missed a spot.*

Climbing in through that window was the most exercise I'd had since the last time Kyle persuaded me to go hiking. Weeks ago. *Ugh. Kyle.* I shook my head to clear that thought.

Stepping out of the bathroom, I stood for a moment between the two bedrooms, the one Billy and I shared to my left and another to my right. I walked forward into the combination living room and kitchen. The afternoon sun provided enough light to see, which was good because I flicked the light switch, and nothing happened. No power. No water. Getting the cabin ready for winter, I assumed. The pot-bellied stove stood to my left and the refrigerator to the right.

I opened the fridge and gagged again. No power meant rotting leftovers. A box with a moldy piece of pizza, a shriveled-up half a roasted chicken that nobody had bothered to wrap up, and something slimy and green that might have been a vegetable at one time. Hard to tell. Miscellaneous plastic containers of mysterious contents, all in various stages of growing penicillin.

I shut the fridge door and opened the small freezer above it. A couple of lumps wrapped in plastic floated in water. One lump had an eye. I hoped it was a fish. I closed the freezer.

I turned toward the living room, looking at the couch. The police report said Billy died on that couch. The cushions had been removed; I didn't want to think about why.

I sighed and whispered into the silence. "Oh, Billy. How did this happen?" Grief clutched at my throat. I swallowed hard and turned away from the couch. I took a few shuddering breaths, counting to four in through the nose, then out my mouth for six—the calming pattern I'd learned in one of Tansy's yoga classes. After a minute, the wave of sorrow passed.

I took the small key from my pocket and asked it aloud, "Okay, little key. Where is your little lock?"

I opened cupboard doors and drawers, looking for anything that locked. The cupboards held plates, bowls, glasses, and cups. No secrets.

I moved to the three drawers below the counter. Silverware in the first, utensils in the second, and dishtowels in the third. I reached my hand inside each, checking for anything hidden.

In the back of the towel drawer, my hand found paper. My heart skipped a little as I pulled it out. Another note for me? A secret document? A clue? No. A manual for the toaster.

Seriously, Billy? Who keeps the manual for a toaster? Duh. Put bread in. Push lever down. Wait. Not rocket science. Snarky Me was being pretty nasty. Nice Me piped up. Don't speak ill of the dead. Another surge of sorrow. More deep breaths.

My search so far had yielded no little locked boxes.

I moved to the sink, which was filled with a week's worth of dirty dishes. I glanced out the window above the sink. The sun was lower in the sky; I'd run out of light soon. I opened the cupboard under the sink, bending over to peer inside. A can of Comet cleanser, half a bottle of Dawn dishwashing liquid, and a plastic ice cream bucket with a plunger in it.

I straightened up and opened the last cupboard door above the fridge. Nothing there but a can of Folger's. I opened the can and dug my fingers into the remaining coffee. People hid stuff in their coffee on TV mysteries. Maybe I'd watched too many of them. Nothing there but coffee. I put it back in the cupboard.

I turned to the stove. I expected an oven caked with burned-on debris and burners crusted with grime. The stove did not disappoint, offering up crust and grime but no secrets.

Billy was a terrible housekeeper. And Amanda too. She'd lied about cleaning the place. What was she doing here? Since she'd locked the cabin, she probably assumed I'd just be looking around outside. *Surprise, Amanda. Gotcha.*

In the fading light, I did a quick check of one bedroom, running my hands under the edges of the mattress on the double bed—another trick I'd learned from TV detectives. I looked under the bed, checked the empty closet and the nightstand. Nothing. No little boxes. No little locks.

I moved to the doorway of the other bedroom and paused. This was the room Billy and I had shared, and judging from the rumpled bedding, this was the room Billy had been using. I wondered for a moment if he ever thought about us as he lay there, if he ever dreamed of me. I swallowed hard. *Get a grip.*

I walked to the nightstand and checked the drawer, where I found a copy of what AA people call "The Big Book." I sat in one AA meeting after Dr. Angela had encouraged me to go and quickly realized that I didn't belong there; these people had serious problems. My problem, if I even *had* a problem, was not that bad. I never went back.

I shook the book, hoping for a secret message to fall out. A "One Day at a Time" bookmark fell out. *One day at a time, Billy, until there are no more days.* I shook the book again, and something fell to the floor. I picked it up. It was me. Well, my senior picture, the wallet size I'd given to Billy senior year. On the back, I had written, "Love you forever, M."

I slipped the photo into my back pocket and sat on the edge of the bed as the dam broke. I sobbed for Billy, for our young selves, for the pain, for the past. For the love. For the loss.

After several minutes, I gathered myself, went into the bathroom, and turned on the cold tap. Nothing. I remembered the water was turned off. I wiped my face on the sleeve of my sweatshirt, grabbed what was left of the toilet paper, and blew my nose. I looked at my reflection in the mirror, a vague resemblance to the younger me in that picture.

Where are you, girl? Who are you now? Not a widow, technically. What are you when you lose someone you used to love? Who were we to each other? A fragment of song popped into my head. "Now you're just somebody that I used to know . . ."

"Stop it!" I said aloud to the girl in the mirror. What difference did it make? No difference at all. I had loved Billy in the past, and now he was gone. Boom. Done.

I went back to his bedroom to finish my search. Nothing under the edges of the mattress. I opened the closet door. His clothes. I leaned in and inhaled. Billy. Don't they say that smell memories are the strongest? I squeezed my eyes shut. *Focus, girl. Keep going. It'll be dark soon.*

I checked the closet floor, the shelf, and pockets in the clothing. Nothing. Nada. Zip.

The cabin ceilings were high and peaked, so no attic to check. I had no desire to go skulking under the cabin in the crawl space since I had no idea what might be skulking under there, waiting for me. Snakes, maybe. Or spiders. Or even an angry chipmunk. I'd seen that one scurry away when I arrived. There might be a whole army of them under there. *Brrr.* I'd have to come back and check the crawl space another time. In the daylight. With some bug killer. Maybe some mace. Which I didn't have but maybe should get. One chipmunk wasn't so bad, but an army of them could cause serious bodily harm.

The sun was lower in the sky. I'd spent longer in the cabin than I thought, checked all I could, and came up with nothing but a sackful of sadness. I went back into the bathroom. The medicine chest held a bottle of Advil, a toothbrush and paste, a mini bottle of mouthwash, and a prescription bottle. Billy's antacid medication. He'd always had a dicey stomach.

Take the bottle, Rational Me said. Billy's death had been ruled an overdose. Nobody bothered to check if this medication was what it claimed to be. Somebody should. *Tag, you're it.* I shoved the bottle into my jeans pocket.

In the mirror, I noticed the shower curtain rod on the shower stall. People hide things inside shower rods, according to TV mysteries. I took the rod down, unscrewed the end cap, and tipped the rod. Nothing came sliding out. No secret messages from Billy. I replaced the rod. No sense in leaving more mess than was already here.

Satisfied there was nothing more to check inside the cabin, I managed to work myself back out of the bathroom window without breaking my neck. I pulled the window down, leaving it open a little bit, just as I'd found it. I hung the screen back up and, using a little stick, coaxed the hook back into place. The only evidence of my being here was the tiny tear in the screen and the wood pile. Nobody would probably notice the screen, but the woodpile was obvious.

I hauled the logs back to the front of the cabin, finishing the task just as the sun dropped behind the trees on the far shore.

I walked to the edge of the lake and stood thinking as the last sunlight sparkled across the water. *Could you have left me a little more to go on, Billy?*

A loon on the lake offered up its haunting cry, calling to its mate, waiting for an answer. I could call from now till the end of time and there'd be only my own empty echo. *Goodbye, Billy,* I whispered into the twilight, then got in my car and headed back to the motel.

LATER THAT NIGHT, I SAT IN bed, nibbling the rest of the pistachios and more Nips, washing them down with Diet Coke as I tried to finish the logic problem I'd started the night before. Which man and which woman shared which activity and on which day? Did Emma Jones and George Smith go kayaking on Tuesday? Or did Laura Peters snorkel with James Andrews on Thursday?

I didn't care. A real-life logic problem rattled around in my brain.

Did Billy die of an overdose, as the autopsy indicated? Had he been clean and sober as Stella hoped and then relapsed as Ben thought? If so, was the overdose accidental or deliberate? Or did someone "off him" as Walter feared? If so, who?

And what about Billy's friends? Did Andy have anything to do with anything, and who was the father of her baby? Billy?

Walter? Joe? Maybe it was immaculate conception. And who was this "Box" guy, and where was he?

Amanda told me she'd cleaned the cabin, but that was a bald-faced lie. Dirty dishes in the sink. And that refrigerator was disgusting. And the toilet. *Ugh!*

I looked at the prescription bottle I'd set on the motel dresser. Was it his stomach medication or something else? Who could tell me?

And the big questions: Where did Billy get the big wad of cash? Why did he give it to me? And what the heck did this stupid key open?

This all felt beyond my capacity to figure out, especially at night. Maybe the morning would give me some answers. I gave up, turned out the light, and fell into a restless sleep.

CHAPTER FIFTEEN

Thursday, October 25

N O HEADACHE THE NEXT morning. What a nice surprise. I needed to talk with Stella about the money. I debated whether to go back and check the cabin's crawl space. I dressed in the previous day's outfit—jeans, sweatshirt, and my running shoes. I turned my undies inside out. Note to Bob: pack more underwear.

I was hungry. I headed to Slim's. Maybe Andy was working again. Maybe she'd tell me more about her relationship with Billy. If there was a relationship.

I stepped out of my motel room door. A skinny guy leaned against my car, smoking a cigarette. He saw me, took a final drag, and flicked the butt out into the parking lot.

"You Mackenzie?"

"Who's asking?" I tensed.

"My old man said you were looking for me."

Ah. The mysterious Box. "You're Eric Boxleitner?"

"Yeah. Everyone just calls me Box." He offered a smile that

was more of a gap-toothed grimace. And the remaining teeth were not in good shape. Meth addict? Or just bad dental hygiene? Hard to tell. Rude to ask.

"How'd you find me?"

He shrugged. "Small town. So, what did ya need?"

I asked him what he thought about Billy's death.

"Oh, man," he said, shaking his head. "That was such a downer."

"What do you think happened?"

"What happened?" Eric sounded just like his father now. "What do you *think* happened? He OD'd, man. He just OD'd. That's what happened. End of story."

"But I heard he'd quit using, that he was sober."

"Yeah, that's what people want to believe, but you can't always believe what you hear, or see either. Trust me. Billy couldn't leave it alone. He just couldn't."

Okay, so Eric voted for OD. "I met Andy at the café. Were she and Billy a couple?"

Eric snorted. "You mean, is he the baby daddy?"

"Well, was he?"

"Oh, she wanted them to be together. She acted like they were, always touching him, wanting to hang out. But he just wasn't into her. At least, I don't think so, but you never know. Behind closed doors, you know?"

At that moment, a Deerwood Police squad car cruised past the motel. We both saw it at the same time. Eric turned away from the street, ducking his head down as he mumbled, "Gotta go. Good luck." He shoved his hands into the pockets of his hooded sweatshirt, walked quickly to the end of the building, and disappeared around the corner.

The squad car rolled on as I got into my car. Box didn't know much. Billy and Andy may or may not have been a couple. Box seemed sure Billy had overdosed. Maybe he was Billy's supplier— if Billy had indeed relapsed. I smacked my hand against the steering wheel. "Damn it, Billy! What the hell happened?"

I was getting nowhere. And I was starving. I headed to the café.

ANDY WASN'T AT SLIM'S. THE CRANKY guy in the tee shirt wasn't there either, but I noticed a tall girl, who looked to be in her late teens, working the grill. An older woman wearing a hair net and a name tag that said Betty came to my table.

"What'll ya have, Doll?"

Oh. My. Gosh. Doll? And Eddie had called me Toots. Had I stepped through a time warp into the 1940s? I wanted to tell her, "Call me Dot and bring me that Adam and Eve thing." But I didn't say that. I ordered French toast and coffee. And a double order of bacon. I love bacon.

I finished my meal and ordered a coffee to go. Betty put it into a paper cup and popped a lid on it. No café grande latte mochaccino frappa-frills here. Just coffee. Black. Or if you really want to dress it up, empty a couple of little plastic creamer thingies into it. And nothing fancy like French vanilla-flavored creamer. Just straight up half-and-half.

Before I left, I kept my voice casual and said to Betty, "I was sorry to hear Billy Stone died. Did you know him?"

She thought a moment and said, "Didn't know him, no. But I guess I did hear something about that. Overdose, wasn't it? I think that's what I heard." I thanked Betty and headed out. Word gets around in small towns.

Going to my car, I called Stella and got her voicemail again. I left a message that I'd try again later.

I decided to pay a visit to Stone Enterprises. Maybe I'm just a nosy person, but the idea that Miss Taylor just left like that bugged me. I hoped to catch Jim in the office and ask him about her. None of my business, I know.

Okay, I am definitely a nosy person.

A twenty-something blonde woman sat at the reception desk, reading a magazine and chewing the nail on her index finger. The office was quiet, other than the sound of a fan blowing and the faint sound of machinery operating somewhere in the back of the building.

I approached the desk, and she gave me a look that clearly said I was interrupting something far more interesting than whatever I had to say.

"Can I help you?" I recognized her as the girl Eddie was talking to, most likely hitting on, at Jim and Stella's the day before. I introduced myself and mentioned seeing her at the house. "Okay," was all she said.

"Is Miss Taylor around?" I knew she wasn't, but I wanted to hear what Blondie had to say. Her eyebrows lifted, almost imperceptibly, but crack sleuth that I am, I noticed.

"Nope. She retired."

"Well, good for her. Is she still in this area, or has she gone somewhere warm?"

Blondie shrugged and got snippy. "How should I know? She was gone before I got here. Is there anything else? 'Cuz I'm kinda busy."

"I can see that," I said, without a single trace of sarcasm, I swear, because my mother taught me to be polite even when someone else is being obnoxious. "Is Jim around? I need to ask him something."

She rolled her eyes. "He's gone to the city today. Don't know when he'll be back." She went back to reading her magazine. We were done. No question.

"Thanks for your help," I said, this time with more than a trace of sarcasm, then turned to walk out. As I reached the door, a middle-aged man in a lab coat stepped around me from behind to open it.

"Allow me," he said and walked out with me. "Nice to see you, Mackenzie. Remember me? Ray Stevens? We met at a company picnic a while back."

I studied his face. Nope. No recollection. Jim had dozens of employees, and those picnics were years ago. And there was lots of drinking, which results in lots of foggy memories all mushed together. *Geez, how much did I drink at those things?*

Ray extended his hand, and I shook it. "Sorry about Billy. And sorry about Mia back there. She can be—well, you saw what she can be."

So Little Miss Perfect had a perfect little name. Mia.

Ray cleared his throat. "Uh, I heard you in there, asking about Miss Taylor. She wasn't planning to retire. Never said a word about it."

So, everyone called Miss Taylor *Miss Taylor*, even her coworkers. I said, "Strange, isn't it? She was here forever. The place revolved around her, or so it seemed."

"Yup, and then one day, she was just gone. No word from her since, that I know of. Everyone, including Jim, was just shocked by her sudden exit."

"Any idea what happened?"

"Well, I don't like to gossip . . ." In my experience, anyone who starts a sentence like that is exactly the kind of person who likes to gossip. And Ray was. "One theory is that she found out something she shouldn't have found out, and somebody paid her a big chunk of change to keep quiet. And she decided to take the money and run."

Hmm. Old Walter had said he thought Billy had "something on somebody." Was there a connection? "Have you heard other theories?"

Ray smiled. "Yeah, that she met a guy online and ran off with him."

I thought about that. Miss Taylor was in her fifties when I saw her last, tall and angular, not a beauty but a pleasant woman. I smiled at the thought of her finding romance and adventure after decades in this little town, working the same job, day after day, year after year. After year.

"She's gone, just like that?" I snapped my fingers.

"Yep. Gone. Nobody's seen her. My wife works the pharmacy at the drugstore, and Miss Taylor hasn't renewed—um, she hasn't been in lately."

"Huh. Do you know if she has family, Ray?"

"I think she has a sister over in Crawford." Crawford, an even smaller town, was about twenty miles from Deerwood, as I recalled.

"Thanks, Ray. Good to see you again."

"You too, Mackenzie. And I was real sorry to hear about Billy. He was a good guy. He used to stop into the shop whenever he came by. Interested in what we were doing. Jim talked about wanting Billy to come into the business someday, you know that 'Stone and Son' kind of thing."

"Yeah, Billy's dad was pretty disappointed he became a cop instead."

Ray gave me that sad, tilting-the-head look of pity. "But Billy had his troubles, didn't he? Anyway, I know Miss Taylor was particularly fond of him. They even went out to lunch a few times. Oh, yeah. That's another rumor that was going around, that there was something going on between them. But that's just ridiculous. She was old enough to be his mother."

I wrinkled my nose. "Ridiculous, yes." I thanked Ray again and left.

All I knew for certain was that Miss Taylor had left abruptly for parts unknown. Had she uncovered some secret? Stone Enterprises makes fishing and hunting equipment. Nothing sinister about that.

And hanging around his father's business didn't sound like Billy; he'd never wanted to become the "and Son" there. But it had been a while since we were together, and people do change. Maybe he saw joining his dad as a quick way to a future. Billy was usually open to taking the easy way out.

But Miss Taylor leaving without a trace? Something wasn't right. And I needed to know if there was any connection with Billy. I just needed to know.

Nosy. Definitely nosy.

CHAPTER SIXTEEN

DEERWOOD IS LIKE A bajillion other small towns in America: if you want to know anything about anyone, ask the clerk at the local drugstore. I hoped Cammy was working. She was.

I set my basket on the checkout counter. Cheese sticks, beef jerky, an almond Hershey, and two boxes of Nips.

Cammy laughed. "Can't ever have too many Nips, right?"

I laughed and then asked, "What do you know about Miss Taylor leaving town?"

She raised her eyebrows. "Why are you asking?"

"Because I'm nosy." I said and laughed again to let her know it was no big deal. Just me being nosy. "I stopped by Stone Enterprises, and nobody seems to know where she went or why. I'm just curious. I mean, why does somebody do something like that?"

Cammy shrugged. "Who knows? There were just rumors at the time. That was, like, a long time ago."

"Uh, Cammy, it was three months ago."

She frowned. "Seriously? Oh, my gawd. It seems like it's been, like, forever."

"What were the rumors?"

She scrunched up her face. "Let's see. I think I heard she was in trouble, like stealing money, embezzling or something, and that's why she bailed." She shrugged. "I just remember my mother saying it seemed fishy when I told her." She laughed. "'Fishy.' My mom thought that was hilarious. You know, because they make fishing stuff?"

Hilarious. I chuckled. "I get it. Can you text me if you think of anything else? You still have my cell?"

She nodded, finished bagging my stuff, and as she handed me the bag, I said, "I especially want to know if Miss Taylor's leaving has anything to do with Billy's death."

Cammy stopped. She frowned. "What could Miss Taylor have to do with Billy's death?" She fidgeted with the display of gift cards on the counter.

"There's probably no connection at all, but doesn't it strike you as odd? She just walks away from her job, this town, her family, and nobody seems to know what happened?"

"Yeah, it's weird, but I don't know what happened. Honest." She made eye contact then, and I read sincerity in her expression.

I said goodbye as another customer came to the register and Cammy got busy. I went outside. Miss Taylor disappears without a trace. Her leaving may or may not have been "fishy." Or she may have run off with some guy she met online. And she and Billy may or may not have had something going on. *Ew.*

I decided another night in Deerwood was in order. I started my car, and as I drove back to the motel, I called the Victorian.

Gram answered. "You'd better get back here," she said.

"What's the problem?"

"Your mother is having a breakdown. She's freaking out!"

Oh geez. Now what? "What's happened?"

"Geez Louise, it wasn't my fault!" Gram said. "I was only trying to get the dryer to work." Gram's ancient gas dryer had been repaired so many times we'd lost count. "If I'd known that was going to happen, I would have moved those other things away from the thing. I didn't know it would catch fire."

"Fire? Oh my God! Is everyone okay, Gram?"

"It's out now. It was just a little fire."

"Where was the fire?"

"Those rags. And that cleaning stuff. Your mother keeps yelling at me that I should have known that stuff was flammable. And I keep telling her that, of course, I knew. But I didn't know there was going to be a fire in the dryer, so it's not my fault."

I could hear my mother in the background, hollering. When she gets anxious, she either starts crying or yelling. I don't know which one is worse.

Gram continued, "Can you hear her? She's been doing that for the last hour! She's gone off the deep end!"

"Let me talk to her, Gram."

Gram laid the phone down with a clunk and called my mother, who continued to holler the whole time she was walking toward the phone. Her first words to me: "That woman is going to be the death of me if I don't kill her first!"

I let her rant for a couple minutes, about how Gram had lost the sense God gave her, and how my mother never knew what she was going to find when she walked in the door. She then started in on Nathan and all the trouble he brought into her life. She suddenly stopped talking. I heard her exhale loudly, and then she said, "Oh well. Nothing can be done about it now. What did you need, Mackenzie? When will you be home? Did you want to come to dinner tonight? The smoke is starting to clear."

My mother's rants usually went on longer. Maybe she was getting less anxious over time. One could hope.

I explained that I would be staying another night in Deerwood. "Could you please—pretty please—run over to my apartment and feed the birds?"

She said she would. "I need to get out of here anyway. Maybe I'll just sleep at your place tonight."

"Not a bad idea. Feel free. Take care of yourself, Mom," I said and disconnected. That house was a zoo sometimes.

CHAPTER SEVENTEEN

B ACK AT THE MOTEL, I did a Google search on my phone for the name Taylor in the area, but nothing promising showed up. I'd have to go old school. In the nightstand drawer, I found a Bible with "Placed by the Gideons" embossed in gold on the cover and next to that, a skinny phone directory.

An actual printed phonebook. Big cities used to have thick telephone directories. I smiled, remembering little sister Deanne perched on the phonebook at the dinner table, back when we lived in the city.

Places like Deerwood have skinny directories. This one was a half-inch thick and covered six little towns, including Crawford. I opened to the *T* section. These would be landlines. No guarantee that Miss Taylor or her family still had one, but I thought I'd try.

There were four Taylors listed. Since I didn't know Miss Taylor's first name, I started calling. I got voicemail on the first two, a recorded man's voice both times. There was no answer at all on the third.

The fourth number rang a few times, and then a woman answered softly, hesitantly, "Hello?"

"Is this the Taylor residence?"

"Yes," she said. I explained that I was trying to reach the Miss Taylor who used to work for Jim Stone. Silence. I waited.

"I'm not . . . I don't know . . ." She hung up. I called back, but the phone rang and rang. I jotted the address on a piece of notepaper with a faded motel logo on it. I got back in my car, checked the map, and headed to the Taylor residence. If the woman was hesitant to talk on the phone, maybe she'd talk to me in person once she saw how non-threatening I was.

Twenty-five minutes later, I knocked on her door, which was met by a barrage of ferocious-sounding barking from inside the house. I didn't need another canine encounter and was just about to run back to the car when the door opened a sliver. A tiny, ancient face appeared in the crack.

"Miss Taylor?"

"Who are you? What do you want?" Her voice quavered, barely audible over the dog noise.

I gave her my name. "Is there a big dog here?" I asked as the barking continued. I didn't want to meet Cujo on this porch.

"Just Duchess," she said. At that moment, a tiny, as in minuscule, dog—a fluffy dust mop with legs, actually—squeezed out through the opening and started sniffing my shoes. No Cujo. I leaned over and petted the fluff. It licked my hand.

"Hello, Duchess," I said. The back end of the mop wagged. A lot of folks believe that dogs can sense if a person is good or evil. I guess I passed the Duchess test because the door swung wider, and the old woman waved at me to follow her inside. I obeyed and waited while she tapped a code into a box on the wall to stop the barking.

She turned to me, gesturing toward the alarm box. "We had that installed a while back. Just to discourage ne'er-do-wells who think two women are vulnerable. I told my daughter we don't need the dog barking when I've got my twelve-gauge at the ready." She waved a hand toward an old armchair, and sure enough, a shotgun was propped beside it.

I'd stepped into a time warp. The 1970s filled the small house—yellow and orange flowered wallpaper, faded with the years, with accents of avocado green. Someone's collection of ceramic mushrooms filled a wall shelf. A dozen or so macrame plant hangers held spider plants and trailing philodendron. A giant ivy plant spilled from the top of a glass-front buffet.

"I like your décor," I said.

"It's all my daughter's doing."

"Ah, your daughter who worked at Stone Enterprises?"

She gave me a confused look. Just then, I heard a door open farther into the house. A voice called, "Mother?"

"Here she is now."

A younger woman, mid-fifties maybe, came into the living room. She was the image of the Miss Taylor I remembered. She eyed me with suspicion until I explained who I was. "I'm just trying to figure out what happened to Billy."

"How would I know?"

"I thought maybe since you worked at Stone—"

She held up a hand. "Oh no. I'm Hannah. You're looking for my sister Helen. *Aha! Miss Taylor had a first name!* At the mention of it, Hannah's mother gave a little sigh. Hannah turned toward her and said, "Mother, I left the groceries on the kitchen counter. Could you put them away, please?"

The older woman shuffled off toward the back of the house, and when she was out of earshot, Hannah continued. "Helen lives next door. A few months ago, she started talking about moving somewhere warm. Then one day, she just up and left, taking all her things. No note. No explanations. I haven't heard a word since."

"How awful for you. And for your poor mother."

"Oh, Mother doesn't know. When she asks about Helen, I say she's at work or had to go out of town. Mother doesn't remember so well these days." I thought of Gram calming Nathan down with what she calls "fiblets." Gram says, "It's kinder that way."

Hannah went on. "When Helen said she was moving somewhere warm, I told her that was ridiculous. There's no place that would be better than being here in Crawford. Our life is here." She scowled. "Who wants to be a lonely old woman sitting on a beach full of strangers? No thanks!" Her expression softened, sadness playing across her face. "And then one day, she was gone. Just gone."

Hannah Taylor went on to explain that the sheriff concluded, since she'd taken clothing and personal items, that Helen left of her own accord. A clerk at Deerwood Drugs, where the Greyhound bus picks up passengers, said she'd boarded the Greyhound headed for Chicago one afternoon, and that was that. No foul play, just as Ben had said.

I wrote my name and cell number on the back of the motel notepaper where I'd jotted the address. "Please call me if you hear from your sister? I'm sure her friends at Stone would like to know she's okay too." And I wanted to know if there was any connection between Miss Taylor's disappearance and Billy's death. The timing just seemed weird.

"One last thing. Did your sister ever talk about Billy?"

Hannah thought a moment. "No, I don't recall Helen mentioning him, but she didn't share much about her life at work."

I thanked Hannah Taylor and left. I drove back to the Deerwood 8, stopping at the gas station to grab a plastic-wrapped turkey and cheese sandwich and a bag of Doritos. I grabbed an apple too. I like to eat healthy.

CHAPTER EIGHTEEN

I CAME OUT OF A deep sleep to pounding on the motel room door. I squinted at the bedside alarm. Almost midnight. How long had I been sleeping? The pounding went on. "Who is it?" I yelled.

"It's me, Stella." Stella? What was she doing out and about at this late hour? Billy's parents were "early-to-bed, early-to-risers," and Billy and I used to joke about that. Can't call them after seven at night. But they loved to call us at seven in the morning. *Ugh. How rude.*

I stumbled to the door. Stella rushed in. "Oh, Mackenzie, I'm sorry to disturb you. Were you sleeping?" *Seriously? PJs? Time? Rumpled bed? Duh.* "Well, I'm glad you're awake. This couldn't wait until morning."

Stella sat in the desk chair, and I sat on the edge of the bed. "What couldn't wait?"

Stella's chair squeaked as she leaned forward, frowning. "You stopped by Stone today," she said, in her you-stole-my-clock tone of voice.

"How do you know?"

"I saw you."

I felt my defenses rising. "Well, what were *you* doing there?" Dumb question, and I knew that as soon as it was out of my mouth.

She shot me an I-can't-believe-you'd-ask-such-a-dumb-question-look and said, parsing out the syllables, "It's *our* business. What were *you* doing there?"

Looked like we'd be playing twenty questions, and I was getting crankier by the minute. "Why does it matter?"

"Why did you have to go over there, upsetting everyone?"

"Everyone? I didn't even talk to or see 'everyone,'" I said.

"People were upset. Nobody likes it when strangers come asking questions."

"Stella, I'm not a stranger. You and Jim were my family. Billy and I knew lots of people at the business. Who was upset, exactly?"

"I'd rather not say, but I would strongly advise you not to be going over there and upsetting people. Our son just died," she said with an emphasis on "our," letting me know I was no longer part of the family or the business. She went on. "Everyone feels awful about that. Nobody needs you over there, causing everyone more grief."

*Every*one again. Who'd told whom that I was there? I'd only seen Mia and Ray. "Stella, I didn't upset *any*one. I was only there a couple minutes."

"Well, I'd appreciate it if you stayed away!" She'd almost shouted.

The thing is, the more people tell me not to do something, the more I think I should do it. And I know that a person is supposed to say yes when they mean yes, and no when they mean no. But there are moments in life when I find it expedient to say yes when I really mean "no way, not a chance." This was one of those times.

"Okay, Stella. I don't want to upset *everyone.*" I made that promise, but I promised myself I'd be doing some more digging at the first opportunity. I had information sources of my own—Cammy, maybe Ray Stevens, or Hannah Taylor. Maybe even Frank.

She let out a sigh and stood up, leaning against the dresser. "Oh, thank you, Mackenzie dear. I knew you'd understand. I'll let you get back to sleep now."

"Yeah, I'm beat. I'll come by tomorrow about the money."

"Just call me to set up a time." Her voice went soft. "It was such a lovely service yesterday. I think William would have approved, don't you?"

I nodded. *Yeah, yeah, lovely. How long was she going to stand here making small talk?* I yawned and stretched.

She took the hint. "You look exhausted, dear. Go back to bed." And with that, she left.

I locked the door after her, then sat for several minutes in the squeaky chair, wondering how my stopping by Stone had upset anyone, let alone "everyone." I was too tired to think about it, so I crawled back into bed and was asleep before I knew it.

CHAPTER NINETEEN

Friday, October 26

QUESTIONS RUMBLED THROUGH MY head the next morning as I dressed in yesterday's clothes. Again. (Note to self: you really need to pack more undies.)

What in the world got Stella riled up enough to come out in the middle of the night to talk to me? Where was Miss Taylor? When someone retires, people say, "Yes, she retired and lives in Florida now." Or she's traveling around the world. Or she moved to the city, or the country, or moved in with her son. Something. Somebody knows something. But in Miss Taylor's case, nobody, not even her sister, who was her next-door neighbor and maybe her best friend in the world, seemed to have a clue as to her whereabouts.

Or maybe Hannah Taylor did know where Miss Taylor was and wanted to protect her for some reason. Ah. This was a sinister new twist. Was Miss Taylor in danger and her sister was trying to ensure her safety with silence?

I thought about my older sister Stephanie, who worked as

an investment adviser in the city. Did I know anything about her life? Did I know her friends, her habits, or her dreams? Or my brother Robbie in LA? I only knew the kid brother he used to be, but who was grown-up Robbie? Or big brother Greg? What do we actually know about others' lives—their daily thoughts, worries, plans?

I didn't know enough about any of my siblings to call and ask, "Hey, how did that thing (event, procedure, interview) go yesterday?" Other than youngest sister, Deanne, who gave the family frequent updates on the impending birth of baby number four, I knew very little about anyone.

Are we all just so absorbed in our own little worlds? Maybe this was the natural progression of life, to grow apart. I suddenly felt sad, then heard Gram's voice in my head, "If you don't like it, change it!" I promised myself to get more interested in my siblings when I got back home.

Ugh. Too much thinking for first thing in the morning.

This was Friday. I had a hot date with Frank in Three Rivers. I had expected to be home before this, but that's the way things work out sometimes.

Before I headed home from Deerwood, I wanted to check under the cabin, the one space I hadn't explored. I figured I had just enough time to do that, get the money from Stella, and get back home in time for Frank. Allowing for an hour or two of primping and preening, doing whatever I could to enhance my natural, um, okay-ness.

As I packed Bob, I remembered Ray Stevens mentioning that his wife worked at the drugstore. Maybe she could tell me what was in Billy's prescription bottle. I looked at the dresser top. The bottle was gone. I checked the bathroom. Not there.

The bottle had been on the dresser last night. I was sure of it. I checked under the bed; maybe I'd dropped it. Then it hit me.

Stella. She must have taken it. Why? Huh. I guess I wasn't the only "thief" around.

I checked out of the Deerwood Super 8, hoping to never see the place again. I'd heard scratching in the walls and ceiling, which I can tolerate. But that morning, one corner of a box of Nips was chewed through. Make annoying noises in my walls? Fine. Eat my Nips? I'm done!

I headed back to the cabin, calling my mother as I drove.

"Those birds of yours are fine," she said with a note of disappointment. "They sure do squawk a lot. You should find a quieter pet." I said nothing. She went on. "I don't know how you sleep on that mattress. You deserve a proper bed, Mackenzie." *Ugh.* "And I cleaned your apartment for you. It needed it."

I just cleaned, but um, thanks, Mom.

I called Gram, expecting to leave her a voicemail, but she answered.

"You're up early today," I said.

"Just enjoying some time to myself, eating a donut and reading the latest China Bayles." Gram loves her mysteries. "Nathan's still sleeping. This is the only time I have to myself. Once he's awake, it's constant—well, you know how he is."

Yes, I knew. I was glad Gram was taking a little break from the caregiving challenge. Even though Gram says she tries to see the blessings, I saw that caregiving could be a burden sometimes.

"I'll be home later. I've got a hot date." Gram wanted details, but I told her to enjoy her quiet time and disconnected.

The morning sun shone brightly, portending another warm, dry day. How long could a drought last? The landscape was long past parched. Grasses had dried up months ago. The standing corn looked pathetic, shriveled stalks just waiting to be cut down. Even the trees had surrendered, the last of the dry leaves drooping. I drove past the remains of Maxwell's, down the road to the cabin where I parked with a view of the lake. One last time.

I sat in my car for a few minutes, reviewing my actions of the previous day. Having "broken and entered," I'd checked everything inside the cabin. Only the crawl space remained.

I grabbed the mini flashlight from my glove compartment. My mother gave all us kids little LED flashlights last Christmas, with the encouragement to keep them in our cars "because you never know." My mother is nothing if not consistent.

I walked toward the cabin. I knelt on the dirt, shining the flashlight into the darkness of the crawl space. A pair of little eyes shone back at me. "Hello there, little guy. I come in peace," I said. He, she, or it scurried away. I got down on my hands and knees. "Ready or not, here I come," I said to nobody (I hoped) in particular.

The space was cramped, so I got down on my belly and started wriggling forward. My flashlight illuminated the drain-pipe under the kitchen sink and another under the bathroom. Under Billy's bedroom lay a large lump of something. I scooched closer.

As I moved, I heard a noise to my left. I swung the flashlight toward the sound, and two eyes looked back, bigger than the eyes I'd seen before. The thing hissed at me. I wriggled backward out of the space as fast as I could, ran, and got to my car just as the air filled with *eau de* skunk.

Once in the car, I sniffed my sweatshirt sleeve. Skunk clung to me. I needed to change clothes. I needed clean underwear. I was sick of eating junk food. I needed my own kitchen (not that I cook), and I missed Tweet and Chirp. I missed Gram. I even missed my mother.

I left Stella one more voicemail, letting her know I was heading home to Three Rivers and I'd call her later to discuss "you-know-what." Cryptic. Maybe she'd think I just meant the money, or maybe she'd realize I knew she'd taken the prescription bottle. Let her wonder.

CHAPTER TWENTY

BACK HOME BEFORE NOON on Friday, showered and in fresh clothes, I made myself a couple pieces of toast with butter and strawberry jam. On my top ten list of comfort foods. My tummy full of toasty goodness, I treated Tweet and Chirp to a shower, placing the cage under the kitchen faucet. They bounced in and out of the trickle of warm water, fluffing and preening between dips.

After I'd refilled their seed and water containers and relined the floor of the cage, I hung it back on the stand in front of the living room window. This was a cheery spot, and the parakeets seemed to love it. They nibbled the treat garland I'd attached to the bars for them, giving me happy chirps. I tweeted back. We were home.

Half an hour later, after I'd tidied up, I headed for Gram's. On the way, I stopped into Burger Barn. The manager looked like he was twelve, told me they were hiring, and handed me a paper application. I thanked him and took an order of fries to go.

Billy had left me that cash, but until I could be sure where it came from, I needed to get a job.

Back in the car, Snarky Me asked, *Seriously? Fast food? Why are you so desperate?*

Desperate Me replied, *Yes. I need a job. I have rent to pay and birdseed to buy. And there's nothing wrong with working fast food.*

Rational Me agreed. As Gram says, there's dignity in all work done well.

Snarky snarked, *But you're applying for the jobs that high school kids and retired people usually take. That's pathetic.*

Yeah, I'm pathetic, Pathetic Me said.

You deserve better," someone said. I think it was my mother, using my voice.

I parked behind the Victorian and went in through the kitchen door, always unlocked during the day. Gram says we are a back-door-kitchen kind of family. Not front-door-parlor people.

I called, "Yoo hoo! It's me!" No answer. My mother would be at work, but I figured Gram and Nathan would be home.

Gram's kitchen feels like home to me. The aromas of homemade bread and cookies have soaked into the cheery yellow walls. The curtains on the big window over the sink are yellow with pale green vertical stripes. The backsplash above the counter tops is painted in a checkerboard pattern of white and green squares.

We—Gram, my mother, and I—gave the kitchen a face-lift two years ago. When my mother suggested a tile backsplash, Gram said, "Why bother at this point in my life? Paint is good enough."

My mother argued. "But subway tile is what everyone is doing now."

Gram scoffed. "Subway tile? This ain't New York City!" My mom gave up, always the best choice when Gram has her mind made up.

"Gram? You here?" I called a little louder. I listened and thought I heard a voice far away, coming from outside in front of the house. I opened the front door and called again. "Gram? Where are you?"

I heard the voice clearer then. "Here, Mackenzie! Upstairs!"

I closed the front door and bounded up the staircase. At the top of the stairs, I reached the second-story window that faced the street. A small roof extended over the front porch. There stood my grandmother. On. The. Roof.

She stared in at me as I tried to open the window. It wouldn't budge. "What the heck?" I yelled through the glass. Gram cupped her hand to her ear. "What?"

I yelled louder. "What the heck are you doing out there?"

She yelled back. "I needed to wash the window, so I closed it but then couldn't open it again."

I pushed against the window harder. No luck. "Wait there!" I yelled. Gram shot me a look that said, *Seriously? Where else would I go?*

I ran downstairs and found a can of silicone spray under the kitchen sink and a screwdriver from what my mother fondly refers to as "the junk drawer." That there is only one junk drawer is a shared family delusion; every one of the drawers holds a mess of odds and ends.

I trotted back up the stairs to find Gram yelling from the roof to someone down below. "I'm fine," she was saying. "My granddaughter is going to rescue me." A pause. "Yes, I'm sure, if she ever gets back." Gram noticed me then. "She's here now," she assured the person. I couldn't hear what the stranger said in reply, but Gram laughed and hollered back, "No, I won't let them stick me out here again!"

I shot the spray into the frame above the lower half of the double-hung window, watching it ooze down. Then it occurred to me I hadn't seen Nathan. I ran to their room. Empty.

Returning to Gram, I pushed against the window frame, and with a little encouragement, it slid upward. I took Gram's hand as she climbed back into the house, carrying a plastic bucket that held a squeegee, Windex, and paper towels. I gave her a hug; she felt cold.

"Where's Nathan, Gram?"

"His friend Jack took him to the Senior Center for cards. I figured it was a good time to get some cleaning done. It's so hard to do anything with him around."

"Geez, Gram. How long were you out there?"

"I went out just after *The Price Is Right*. Or maybe it was *The People's Court*." She rubbed her arms and shivered. She'd been out there on the shady side of the house for an hour or more. In short sleeves.

"What would you have done if I hadn't come home?"

"Wouldn't that have been a hoot? Especially if I'd hollered that your mother put me out there on purpose. Somebody would have reported her to the welfare for elder abuse."

"Yeah, a hoot, Gram. Maybe next time, be sure someone is home before you take a chance like that, okay?"

"Oh fiddlesticks, Mackenzie, I can handle those things. I'm not one of those feeble old ladies! Actually, it was kind of nice out there with nobody bugging me, just sitting in the peace and quiet. I might just stick a lawn chair out there and make it my private little retreat. Now I've really gotta tinkle. I was about ready to use that bucket!" She headed toward the bathroom.

"Before I forget, there was a weird phone call earlier. I wrote it down on the . . ." her voice trailed off as she closed the bathroom door.

"On the what?" She couldn't hear me over the sound of running water. Gram always runs the water in the sink while she tinkles.

I headed down to the kitchen and saw a scrap of paper by the phone. In Gram's cramped hand, it read, "Leave it alone." Leave what alone? Who had called?

My stomach growled. Gram's kitchen has that effect. I made myself a turkey sandwich with a little Miracle Whip. Five minutes later, Gram came into the kitchen.

I waved the paper at her. "What does this mean? Who called?"

"I think it was a woman," Gram said. "But I had a feeling they were disguising their voice, so I can't be sure. They just said, 'She needs to leave it alone,' and hung up."

"Did you ask their name?"

"Oh, I wasn't talking to them. It was a message on that answering machine."

"Okay, good. I'll just call your voicemail. Maybe I'll recognize the voice."

"Um, you know, at the end of the message, she says to press this or that? I think I might have pressed the wrong button."

I checked. She had. "Well, Gram, you erased the message."

"Sorry about that."

I tried star-sixty-nine. Nathan's friend Jack had called after the mystery call. "No luck, Gram. It's going to remain a mystery, I guess."

Gram shrugged. "I can't figure out that new-fangled stuff. Life was easier in the old days." Gram got a faraway look and then shook her head and came back from wherever the good old days had taken her. "That sandwich looks good. I got real hungry out there on the roof."

I handed Gram half my sandwich, and we stood there by the cupboard, chewing in silence. *Who had called? Who was supposed to leave what alone?*

Anyone I'd met in Deerwood—Billy's motley crew—had my cell number, not Gram's landline. So, the message couldn't be for me. But who, then? My mother? Gram?

"It was probably a wrong number," Gram said.

I nodded. "Yeah. Probably." I wanted that to be true. Just a wrong number.

"Didn't you say you had a hot date tonight?"

I told her a quick version of meeting Frank in Deerwood, then went back to her risking her neck to wash the window. "Didn't anyone see you on the roof before I got here?"

"Everybody's working. Next time I'll be sure to get stuck out there on the weekend."

"What was your plan if I hadn't come over?"

"Oh, I'd have hollered for one of the neighbors to call the fire department. Wouldn't that have been a hoot—to go down one of those big ladders, with one of those good-lookin' firemen, like on the calendars, carrying me?"

We chewed in silence for a while, lost in our little fantasies.

CHAPTER TWENTY-ONE

FRANK ARRIVED AT PRECISELY seven o'clock on Friday night, which impressed me since Billy was never on time for anything, including our wedding. I told Chirp and Tweet not to wait up and locked my front door.

Frank opened the car door for me. A gentleman, my mother would say. She has much to say about how manners have been lost and how casual dating and hook-ups are the norm with my generation. I assure her I've never been interested in that, but she looks skeptical. Her rants about the lack of "decency and good morals" always get an eyeroll from Gram, who reminds my mother, "You weren't exactly Polly Purebred in your younger days, Barbara."

Gram reminds her, "It has been ever thus. The Bible says so. And kids in ancient Rome were just like kids today. Nothing is different; we just hear about things now. We kept private things private in my day. That was better."

As I settled into the passenger seat, I noticed Mrs. Litowsky was watching from her window. I gave her a little wave. She waved back and then closed her drapes. Frank noticed too. "Nosy neighbor?"

"She watches out for me," I said. "And I watch out for her. And her cat." Chloe is a cat with gorgeous black and white stripes and bright green eyes. She lives outside most of the time in nice weather but makes herself at home with Mrs. L when the mood suits her.

Right-on-time, car-door-opening, chivalrous Frank and I had a lovely meal at the best restaurant in Three Rivers, a little place on River Street called Donatello's. The best Italian food in this part of our state. Or at least that's what Loretta Donatello wants you to think. And I do.

Donatello's is housed in one of the old Victorian storefronts along the river. Inside it offers big-city ambience, as big-city as we get in Three Rivers. The huge fireplace in the dining room adds a warm glow all winter, but it held no fire tonight. With the drought, people in town seemed to be in a holding pattern. Waiting. Waiting for rain. Waiting for the season to change. Waiting for the cold snap we usually had by now, letting us all know it was time to settle in for the coming winter. Maybe we town and city dwellers aren't all that far removed from our cave-dwelling forebears.

Candlelight danced across the polished oak table around the vase with one perfect rose. Ah, romance. Frank ordered wine. I like a man who takes charge, though he did check with me to be sure it was okay. Since I'd already broken my sober streak on Monday, I agreed.

As we shared a plate of stuffed mushrooms, Frank said, "I didn't know Billy very well at all. Just met him once or twice. Tell me about him."

I filled Frank in on my life with Billy. (I know it's not a good idea to talk about your exes on a first date, but, hey, Frank asked.)

"And what's the deal with Eddie? I've seen him around the business, and I saw how he was after the funeral." He made a disgusted face. "Has he always been such a sleaze?"

I gave him the abbreviated Eddie details, then said, "I'd rather not talk about him." Frank shrugged an okay, and as we dug into our entrees (my perfect ribeye, his delicate salmon), he told me more about his life before Deerwood. Never married. No children. Two sisters, both younger. Parents happily married. Average middle class American childhood. No drama. No trauma. Just . . . nice.

"So why did you leave the city? Seems like you had a good life there," I said.

"A good life, yes, but boring. I was ready for a change, some adventure."

"Ha! You picked Deerwood for adventure?"

He smiled. "Adventure is in the eye of the beholder. Fishing, hunting, no commute, no crowds, fresh air. What's not to like? I can leave my office, and half an hour later, I'm in the boat or out in the woods. Like vacation any time I want it. I can walk out my door and be on the trail, hiking or snowshoeing. Five minutes away from paradise, all the time."

I smiled. "Sounds great—if you like that sort of thing."

"You don't?"

I wanted to tell Frank how I much preferred reading to running, how I'd pretended to like things I didn't really like just to hold on to relationships. I wanted to tell Frank that my idea of a good time was watching movies curled up on the couch with a bowl of popcorn. I wanted to be honest, but then I heard my mother's voice in my head with that advice about pretending to like what the guy likes, "if you ever hope to have a boyfriend." So, I stopped talking. I didn't want to ruin the possibility of a future relationship with Frank by being too honest. How cheesy is that?

I changed the subject and told him about stopping by Stone.

"I heard," he said. "You poked the beehive. Got everybody *buzzing*." He chuckled at his own joke.

"*Everybody?*"

He shrugged. "You know how small towns are."

I told him how Stella had come to the motel. "All I did was ask a question about Miss Taylor."

Frank shrugged again. "And nobody has the answer. Not even Jim. Nobody."

Maybe it was the wine, but I felt my cheeks flush. Okay, so not just the wine. Anger. I snapped, "Well, *some*body has the answer. I mean, people don't just disappear off the face of the earth!"

Frank held up his hands in surrender. "Hey, don't get mad at me. I'm just saying it's a mystery. People leave, and they have their reasons. Nobody's business but their own. But if you want to track her down, knock yourself out."

He went back to eating, and I cooled down. What did it matter, really? I was imagining something sinister, and it was probably all just innocent. Frank was right. People had a right to privacy. Miss Taylor must have had a reason to just pack up and leave. End of story.

Maybe Stella was right, I thought as I chewed my steak. Maybe I should just leave it alone. But I had a feeling I wouldn't.

We finished our meal, filling the spaces between bites with idle chatter interspersed with laughter and warm camaraderie.

Frank made an even better second impression than the first, which was already pretty great. Or maybe it was the wine. We finished off the bottle with dessert, splitting an order of Loretta's delectable turtle cheesecake.

Frank paid the check—another truly gentlemanly, and un-Kyle-like, thing to do. As we stepped outside, Frank took my hand. "I don't know Three Rivers. Show me your town?"

We ambled down River Street, hand in hand, past Tansy's yoga studio and then the First Savings Bank building where I used to work; working for Trip at Kipling Financial seemed like another lifetime, not just a few days ago. I directed Frank's gaze across the river to Rawley Park, where I'd gotten dumped by Kyle, again a lifetime ago. Walking on, I pointed out Lou's Vintage, owned by Gram's friend Lou Burgess, and the Oven Fresh Bakery, owned by a friend of my mother's.

After half an hour of ambling, we stopped in at Java Java, which has the best coffee in town. On weekends, local musicians play. A not-too-bad guitarist strummed along as we sipped Java's decaf Starry Night Blend with whipped cream and cinnamon on top. By the time we got back to Frank's car, we'd walked and coffeed ourselves sober.

Frank pulled up in front of my apartment building, leaving the car running. Ah, the moment. Nightcap or no nightcap? I felt suddenly tired.

"Thanks so much, Frank. This was lovely. I'd invite you in, but I'm exhausted. This has been quite the week."

"Oh, I understand. So sorry again about your ex. And your job. And Bangladesh." I cringed. It was a lot to handle in one week. At least he didn't mention my hair.

I imagined for a moment how wonderful it would feel to have Frank wrap me in his arms and then, well, whatever. But before I could say anything that would get me in trouble, Frank spoke.

"I'll let you get some sleep. We can do this again, right?"

"Right. Absolutely." Frank got out and came around to my car door. Wow. This was a level of chivalry you just don't often see anymore. I could get to like this kind of treatment.

He opened the door and extended his hand. I took it and got out of the car. I started to say, "Thank you for a lovely—" but before I could finish, he pulled me toward himself and kissed me. Gently. Very. Gently.

I kissed him back. Slightly. Less. Gently.

I said, "Thanks for a wonderful evening."

He smiled, circled an arm around my waist, and walked me to my door, where he smiled again. "I'll look forward to next time. Good night. Sleep well." And with that, he left.

Later, I lay in bed, smiling. *Geez, if there had been a rain puddle, he'd have thrown his cloak down so I wouldn't have to get my dainty little feet wet. If there had been a dragon, he'd have slain it for me. If there had been . . .* There I was, getting carried away. Frank was a nice guy, yes, but was he really Sir Walter Raleigh, Saint George, and maybe even Sir Lancelot, all wrapped together in a very nice bundle?

Cynical Me whispered, *He sounds too good to be true. Be careful.* I did have a habit of getting myself all worked up when I met a new guy, making him out to be Mr. Wonderful when he might be, in fact, Mr. Less-Than-Wonderful, or in the case of Kyle, Mr. Leaving-You-For-Bangladesh.

Or like Billy, Mr. I'll-Die-and-Leave-You-Wondering. And heartbroken.

Swamped then by a wave of sadness on top of the exhaustion, I slept.

CHAPTER TWENTY-TWO

Saturday, October 27

HALLOWEEN IS A BIG deal here in Three Rivers. All through October, local shops are decked out for the holiday, offering Halloween sales, and there's a parade the Saturday before Halloween. Pretty much everybody in town dresses up in costume, the marchers *and* the spectators. Even the old folks at Drury's Rest, the only nursing home in town, turn out in costume to watch the parade as it goes down River Street past the residence.

The parade ends up at Rawley Park, where the fire department builds a huge bonfire. Even with the fire department in charge, people were anxious this year. The town council debated. Bonfire: yes or no? The consensus finally came down to yes. Even in a drought, Halloween in Three Rivers just wouldn't be Halloween without the bonfire.

Local businesses set up their booths around the fire area, selling hot cider and coffee, cookies, sandwiches, ice cream treats, and other assorted goodies. Witches, goblins, and fairy princesses gather in the park, along with hoboes, superheroes, and, for those who don't plan much ahead, the kid-ghosts in the pillowcases with the eyes cut out.

Kyle and I had planned to attend this year's parade and bonfire together, dressed as Captain Hook and Peter Pan. I wanted to be Captain Hook, but he talked me into being Peter instead. We'd picked up the costumes a couple of weeks ago, and Kyle said he'd hang on to them until today. But that was before Bangladesh entered the picture.

That's why, on Saturday afternoon, with the parade about to start, I scrambled to come up with a costume. I wrapped a red bandana around my hair. I threw on my jeans and turned up the cuffs. I put on my denim shirt, rolled up the sleeves, and tied the tails at my waist. Rosie the Riveter would have to do.

I slipped into my ASICS and rolled white crew socks down to my ankles. I trotted the four blocks down to River Street and found my mother, Gram, and Nathan sitting in lawn chairs outside Lou's Vintage Shop. Lou herself sat next to Gram, wearing a pair of lime green bellbottoms and an orange macrame vest over a purple tie-dyed shirt. She'd tied on a cloth KEEP ON TRUCKIN' headband. Groovy.

Gram saw me and said, "Hi, Rosie!" without hesitation.

"I knew you'd get it," I said, giving her a hug. Gram had pulled her long gray hair into two pigtails, tied them with blue ribbons, and drawn on some freckles. "Who are you supposed to be?" I asked.

"Wendy," she said.

"Wendy, as in Peter Pan?"

She shook her head. "Nope. Wendy as in hamburgers." Ah. The little girl from the Wendy's logo.

Nathan was dressed all in white with a black string tie, his white hair slicked back from his forehead, and a white stick-on mustache and goatee. He smiled at me.

"Hello, Colonel," I said, giving a little salute.

"Evenin', ma'am. Aren't you a delightful-lookin' li'l chicken!" he drawled.

Gram slapped his shoulder. "Behave yourself!"

Nathan winked at me. Gram explained how they were hungry when they decided what costumes to wear.

My mother, in her lawn chair next to Nathan, had painted her face green and wore a black witch hat, black sweater, and black leggings. Snarky Me thought the witch get-up was apropos. Nice Me said, "They're into fast food. What's *your* story?"

She rolled her eyes. "Good grief. My 'story' is that all those two ever think about is eating, and if I don't watch it, I'll weigh a ton living with them. And I found this hat in the attic, and it seemed fitting with how I've been feeling lately. *That's* my story."

I nodded, understanding; my mother had been a little crankier than usual lately. Nice Me said, "Well, you look great."

She scowled, crossed her arms, and sank deeper into her chair. "Whatever." Geez, even the Halloween parade couldn't cheer her up.

I edged past Lou and sat on the curb in front of Gram's lawn chair. She rubbed my shoulders, and I felt the tension of the past week easing.

Gram turned to Lou. "Mackenzie just lost her job."

"I thought she worked for Trip Kipling," Lou said.

"Yes, and that fool let her go!" Gram was indignant.

I jumped to Trip's defense. "It wasn't Trip's fault. The order came down from on high, from his father."

Lou huffed and launched into a diatribe against Big George. "That pompous ass! He thinks he owns the town and everybody in it. Tried to buy the whole block right out from under all of us small business owners. Wanted to turn it into some convention center, or sports place, or some nonsense like that."

"How did you stop him?" I asked.

"We all showed up at the town council and screamed bloody murder, that's how!" Lou flashed a look of triumph. "That put the kibosh on his scheme!"

"You gave him what-for!" Gram said.

"We settled his hash!" Lou said.

Nathan chimed in. "Hash? Is there hash?"

Gram said, "No, dear. No hash. But we can have some when we get back home after the parade."

"Where's the parade?" he asked.

Gram's grip tightened on my shoulders. Drumbeats sounded from just down the block. "It's coming. Just wait. Just wait . . ." She massaged my shoulders so hard I yelped and wiggled away.

Lou spoke. "So, Mackenzie, you need a job, huh?" I turned toward her as she continued. "I've been thinking of hiring someone part-time. I'm getting too old to be working this hard."

I thought it might be okay to have a little job at Lou's where I wouldn't have to worry about much. "What would I be doing?"

"Well, you could start just helping me get things organized in there." She tilted her head to the storefront behind us. I'd been in there, and it was a riot of confusion. Stuff, stuff, and more stuff. Everywhere. And I love sorting and organizing stuff.

"When would you want me to start?"

"Give me a few days to figure things out. Start sometime next week, maybe?"

I didn't even ask about pay since any amount would be more than I was earning at the moment. "Great. Thanks so much, Lou!"

"Hey, I'm not doing you a favor. You'll be helping me, so thank you." She smiled.

I turned to Gram. "You set this up, didn't you?"

She winked at me. "Hush, now. Here's the parade."

We all stood as the color guard from the local VFW marched by. When we were kids, Gram would order us at the start of every parade, "Stand up! The flag is passing by!" An unabashed patriot, my grandmother is as American as can be, and she instilled in her children and grandchildren a love for this country.

I glanced at Nathan, a Korean War veteran, as he saluted the flag and at Gram with her hand to her heart, a tear in her eye. I swallowed hard. America. *My country, 'tis of thee.*

The Three Rivers High School band—about forty kids in all—marched by playing the theme from *Ghostbusters.* Following the band were three convertibles, tops down, bearing signs advertising Larson Motors, the biggest car dealership in town. Seated on the back of each car was a local VIP. Or what passes for a VIP around here. I heard Billy again, with the "big fish, small pond" thing.

Mayor John Dodson rode in the first car, his name spelled out under the Larson Motors logo. Trip's dad sat on the back of the second convertible. The sign read simply BIG GEORGE because everybody in town knows who he is. He waved at the crowd, and Lou blew a raspberry at him.

"That should say BIG JERK!" she hollered. Big George heard it and gave her a creepy smile. "Smug bastard," she muttered.

Gram put her hand on Lou's arm. "It's over now, Lou. You can relax."

"Relax? Ha! How can any of us ever relax when that four-flushing, double-dealing rat is running this town?" She gave a disgusted grunt and fell silent.

I had always thought of Big George as a good businessman. I thought Trip's was the only dissenting opinion. You learn something every day.

The third convertible carried Lisa Arneson, a twenty-something culinary arts student at Wolf Valley Tech. Lisa came in third on a national TV cooking show, which made her pretty much royalty in town. As she rolled by, the crowd offered up applause and some wolf whistles, including a loud one from Nathan.

The Snow Shovel Brigade followed, a dozen or so women scraping the street and swinging shovels over shoulders in synchrony as they sang along to a boombox blasting "Let It Snow" and "Frosty the Snowman." Gram's friend Velma was part of that group.

Gram hollered, "Go, Velma!" Her friend waved her shovel in reply.

The parade went on. The Scouts, a mix of boys and girls these days, marched by, followed by the doggy daycare clients with their pets in costume. The Oven Fresh Bakery's owner, my mother's friend Doris, rolled past in a little car with a giant donut on top. The local Kiwanians marched by dressed as scarecrows.

I sat smiling at it all. How small-town America can we be? Perfectly small-town America, it seemed, and I felt a surge of fondness for this place, these people. Decent, hard-working, kind souls. This was home.

A moment later, I had that neck-prickly feeling someone was watching me. I looked at the crowd around me and then at the people opposite. Just when I thought I was imagining things, I saw him. A guy across the street wearing a black hoodie stared in my direction, his face obscured in shadow. When he saw me looking back, he ducked his head and hurried away. The crowd wasn't enormous, but there were a couple layers of people on that side of the street. I stood up to see where he went, but he'd disappeared into the crowd.

Then someone else across the street grabbed my attention. Captain Hook. Not just any Captain Hook, but Kyle in his Captain Hook costume. The long red coat, black breeches, and black boots. Long, curly, black wig topped by a black hat with the huge white feather. The fake hook hand. Kyle obviously hadn't left for Bangladesh yet. And he'd evidently been ready for our breakup because standing next to him? Yup. Peter Pan. Wearing my Peter Pan costume.

Rational Me said it was none of my business what Kyle was doing since we were no longer a couple, if we had even *been* a couple, which was debatable. But he hadn't wasted any time replacing me. And that stung.

Snarky Me decided that Peter Pan did not look great in my costume. The tights, stretched to the max, looked as though they could explode any minute. And the shoulders on her! Broad shoulders. Very broad. And big biceps bulging under the stretchy green top.

I squinted to get a clearer view. Big biceps, broad shoulders, bulging thighs. *Wait. What?* Five o'clock shadow?

Peter Pan was a guy. Kyle didn't have a brother. Maybe this was a coworker. Yes, that must be it. A coworker. And they were going to a Halloween party after the parade. And *then* Kyle would be leaving for Bangladesh.

Snarky whispered, *Geez. How naïve can you be?*

Rational Me spoke up. *Just let it go, Mackenzie. It's fine. Kyle isn't your boyfriend, remember? What he does is his own business.*

Rational Me was right, of course. Snarky Me couldn't help

but think that I would have been a much cuter Peter Pan. Kyle's loss.

Gram tugged on the back of my shirt. "Sit down! You're blocking my view of the veterans!" I sat down abruptly; Gram says sit, you sit.

The guys from the local VFW marched by, followed by the ladies of the auxiliary, who handed out cards inviting the community to a fundraising chicken dinner the next night at the local VFW post. Buy two dinners, get a third free. I could see it coming.

"Well, looky here," Gram said. "Buy two and get a third free. How 'bout it, Mackenzie? We haven't seen much of you lately. Want to eat some chicken with me and Nathan?"

Sure, Gram, I thought. *I don't have a life anyway, so why not have dinner with my old granny and her old husband?* I didn't say that, of course. I smiled at Gram and said, "Sounds great!"

She said, "Good. 'Cuz you don't have a life anyway, right?" I swear that old woman can read minds.

The parade ended, and the crowd dispersed, some going home, but most making their way over the bridge toward Rawley Park. My phone dinged. A text from Tansy. "Bonfire?"

I texted back and agreed to meet her at the warming house.

Like a lot of parks in this part of the country, Rawley Park has a permanent warming house, a building adjacent to the field the Parks Department floods in December to create an outdoor skating rink. The warming house is just that—a place for ice skaters to warm up between rounds of skating. Warming houses usually smell of sweat and wet wool, but when you're freezing to death, you don't mind.

Tansy was standing outside the little building when I got there, dressed all in black. Black sweater over black leggings, little black boots, pointy black furry ears on her headband and black whiskers drawn on her cheeks. *Meow.* The black tail completed the look, which was adorable. I wished I had a better costume than last-minute Rosie, but, well, Kyle. Enough said.

I told Tansy about seeing Kyle with the ugly Peter Pan. She sympathized. I filled her in on the funeral, the cabin, the key, and the money. She listened and asked me a lot of questions. I had very few answers.

I told her about my date with Frank. She brightened up. "Sounds amazing. You deserve a great guy." I told her she was absolutely right about that. (How come I can accept a "you deserve better" from Tansy but not from my mother? Because, well, mothers.)

Tansy and I had just gotten hot chocolate and a couple of cookies and were walking around the bonfire area when I looked up and saw the guy in the hoodie again. "Hey!" I jostled Tansy's elbow, causing her hot chocolate to slop out onto her sleeve.

"Hey, yourself! You made me spill!"

"There's that guy!"

"What guy?"

"Hoodie Guy!" I pointed toward where I'd seen him. Nobody but parents and kids in sight. I filled her in—how I'd had that neck-prickly feeling at the parade and how he'd ducked into the crowd. And how he was here too and then disappeared again.

"Who is it?" she asked.

"Well, if I knew his name, I could call him that instead of Hoodie Guy."

Tansy frowned. "Okay, some weird guy is stalking you? This is creepy. I'm worried."

Tansy was scared for me. Was *I* scared for me? Not really.

"It's just someone *trying* to scare me. I'm more annoyed than afraid, really. I mean, what's the guy gonna do? Annoy me to death?"

Tansy shook her head. "You don't know who this guy is or what he's capable of. It's okay to be brave, but not okay to be stupid! You never know!"

Tansy's great, but sometimes she sounds like my mother. She continued, "And I don't want you walking home alone in the dark. I'll drive you home. Better yet, come stay at my place tonight."

"Thanks, but I was already gone three nights this week. Tweet and Chirp missed me. But I will take the ride home."

"Do you want me to stay with you? I will, you know."

"Thanks, but I'll be fine." We walked around the park for another half-hour and, despite my insistence that I wasn't scared, I spent a lot of time looking over my shoulder. Rational Me made the argument that he was probably just some random person in a hooded sweatshirt and just coincidentally looked at me when I looked at him. Probably totally innocent, and I was probably overreacting. Probably. Anxious Me was not convinced.

I let Tansy drive me home, and I let her come in to check my closets and make sure no hoodied creeps were hiding in my shower. And I let her double-check that the doors were locked and the windows latched. She closed all my curtains, and I used my broom to tap on the ceiling to let Mrs. Litowsky know I was home. After a few seconds, Mrs. L tapped back. I'd laughed in the past, telling Tansy about this little signal we have. Tonight, it wasn't funny; it was comforting.

"Pays to have a nosy neighbor at a time like this," Tansy said, then hugged me. "Text me in the morning so I know you're safe, okay?" I promised I would.

After she left, I locked and relocked my front door. As I tucked my parakeets under their cage cover, I whispered, "You guys will protect me, won't you?" They made no promises.

CHAPTER TWENTY-THREE

Sunday, October 28

I WOKE LATE SUNDAY MORNING to another sunny day with a cloudless, intensely blue sky. I spent a couple of hours cleaning my apartment. Although I'd already cleaned, and my mother said *she'd* cleaned, I had an urge to dust baseboards, shake rugs, and vacuum under furniture. Why the deep cleaning? Just in case she came over again and criticized my housekeeping. How old do you have to be to stop caring about your mother's approval? Older than I am, evidently.

I also cleaned so I could think. Mindless physical activity helps when I am trying to figure something out. I felt stuck. Not sure how Billy really died, with niggling doubts about the overdose conclusion. No clue what the key meant, where all that money came from, the Miss Taylor thing, and Stella swiping the prescription bottle I swiped from the cabin. And ugh, the dirty cabin. And Kyle. And Hoodie Guy.

When I feel stuck, or frustrated, or hurt, I clean. I organize. I keep my mind busy. Dr. Angela suggested in the past

I might have a bit of OCD. Whatever. I do love a clean and pristine space.

Early afternoon, Mrs. Litowsky rapped on my back door. She wore a blue open cardigan over her green and blue flowered dress. She always wore dresses. Did she even own a pair of pants? I couldn't imagine her in jeans.

"I'm going to the store. Do you neet anything?" Her accent always made me smile. She had one of those little metal carts that you pull along behind you, like a rolling suitcase. Her purse was in the cart.

I pointed at the purse. "Aren't you afraid someone might grab that from the cart?"

"Here? In Three Riffers? Heavens no!" she said. She patted her sweater pocket. "Besides, I've got pepper spray right here. Muggers, beware!"

"Clever, Mrs. L." I assured her I didn't need anything, even though it would have been nice to have something in my fridge besides a shriveled orange and a bottle of mustard. And Kyle's dark beer. As she turned to go, I changed my mind. "Maybe you could grab a loaf of bread for me? The cheap white kind is fine."

"Vite bread? That's no goot for you. I'll get you a nice veet. Or maybe you'd like a rye? Or a pumpernickel? That's the best. Goot fiber for you!"

I didn't want to argue. "Whatever goes with peanut butter," I said. She shook her head and tsk-tsked me. I grabbed a five-dollar bill from the kitchen drawer where I kept my extra cash.

After she left, I stood looking into that drawer. I've spent most of my adult life feeling like I don't have "enough." Not enough education. Not a good enough job. Never enough in the bank. But now, thanks to Billy, I had some money—a lot of money, for me. But was it "enough"? That depended on what I wanted to do with it. And more importantly, it depended on where the money came from.

What if Billy did something dastardly for that money? What if the money came from selling drugs, getting school children high? Was that even possible? Could Billy have changed that much?

Too many unanswered questions. I went back to cleaning. Like a fiend, I cleaned. By mid-afternoon, my apartment sparkled and smelled like Pine-Sol. As Gram says, "It's not clean unless it's Pine-Sol clean!"

I showered. With the squirrel tamed, my hair looked halfway decent. I even slapped on a little blush and ran the mascara through my lashes. I don't wear a ton of makeup, just what's essential for going out. The rest of the time, I'm happy with what God gave me, and when we're young (thirty-five is still young, right?), what God gives most of us is the lovely blush of youth. Now, when I hit my forties, I'm sure I'll feel differently, but for now, minimal makeup is my style.

Gram phoned just after four to let me know she and Nathan would meet me at the VFW. My stomach growled. Chicken dinner was calling.

The VFW Hall has been around since World War II and hasn't had many improvements. A one-story building on Farrell Street, close to downtown, its white clapboard siding is punctuated with a few small windows high on the side walls and a single door in the front. I assumed they had a back door in case of fire.

Stepping inside, I was assaulted by the lingering odors of decades of cigarette smoke and stale beer. The Three Rivers town council outlawed smoking inside businesses years ago, but the smell persisted.

Tables were set around the room. It doesn't matter if it's a VFW chicken feed, a church potluck, or a funeral lunch. Wherever a small-town crowd gathers to eat in this part of the world, you'll find long plastic folding tables covered in white paper cloths.

I joined Gram and Nathan in the buffet line set up along the back wall. I took two pieces of fried chicken and a glob of mashed potatoes, over which I ladled a scoopful of the gravy simmering in a crockpot. I helped myself to a spoonful of peas and carrots, then grabbed a bun from a basket and a couple pats of butter wrapped in gold foil.

A separate buffet table offered pieces of marble cake with a choice of white or chocolate frosting. Next to the cake stood one of those huge coffee urns, which never, ever make good coffee.

I followed Gram and Nathan to a table and sat across from them.

I dug in as if I hadn't eaten in months. Probably because that dinner with Frank Friday night was the only decent meal I'd had recently.

I heard Gram chuckle across the table. I looked up. "Child, slow down. There's plenty here." I wiped a dribble of chicken fat from my chin with my paper napkin. This was the juiciest chicken I'd ever had, I swear.

"I guess I'm just hungry tonight." Before I could say more, the front door of the VFW opened behind Gram. A figure stepped in, the light from outside behind him casting him in shadow. I couldn't be positive, but I thought it might be Hoodie Guy. If so, Tansy was right. I had a stalker. I squinted at him as he stood in the doorway surveying the room. Then he saw me looking at him and turned and ducked back outside.

On my feet in a flash, I headed after him. Unfortunately, just as I got to the door, three men came in, all wearing their VFW hats and vests. I bumped smack into the middle one of the three—a heavy-set, balding guy with Harold on his name tag.

As I bounced off him, Harold reached out and grabbed my arm. I might have hit the floor if he hadn't caught me. "Whoa there, Toots," Harold said with a laugh, releasing me. Second time this week a man called me Toots. *Geez.*

One of Harold's buddies said, "Hot damn, Harold! Women are throwing themselves at you tonight!" The group laughed. I did not. I shot Harold a distinctly un-Toots-like look, scooted around him and out the door. I looked up and down Farrell Street. No sign of Hoodie Guy. Disappointed, I went back inside.

Gram was done with her dinner, and Nathan was polishing off my mashed potatoes. Before I could say something to him like, "Hey! That's *my* food," Gram shot me a warning look, which we all know means, "Remember, Nathan forgets things, so we make accommodations. Be nice." I remembered and smiled at her.

She asked, "For heaven's sake, where did you take off to?" I didn't want Gram to worry. I gave her what I hoped was a reassuring smile and shrugged. "I thought I saw someone I knew, but it wasn't." Gram frowned but didn't say anything more. Nathan finished cleaning my plate and pushed it away. I smiled at him. "Can I get you anything else?"

He scowled at me. "You're a terrible waitress. It's about time you came back to our table. I was ready to leave without giving you a tip! I want some cake. With chocolate frosting."

Gram gave me a pained look and asked if I wouldn't mind getting it. I fetched theirs and grabbed two more pieces for myself. Then I made another trip to get three Styrofoam cups of coffee for us.

When I came back to the table, Nathan looked up and brightened. "Mackenzie! When did you get here?" Gram gave me a sad smile, shaking her head.

Yes. We make accommodations.

CHAPTER TWENTY-FOUR

TRIED TO SLEEP, BUT I saw Hoodie Guy every time I closed my eyes. Who the heck was he? Seeing him more than once in twenty-four hours had to be more than coincidence. And him ducking out of sight each time was downright creepy.

I fell into a fitful sleep sometime after eleven, and later, I dreamed that my older brother Greg was yelling, "Fire! Get out!" In the dream, I smelled smoke and heard the incessant beeping of a smoke alarm. I tried to follow Greg down the hall of the second floor of the house where we grew up. But as is often the case in dreams, I couldn't find my way out. He disappeared into the smoke. I tried to call his name but couldn't make a sound.

I jolted awake. The smoke smell was real.

The kitchen smoke alarm screamed.

I jumped out of bed. The bedside lamp didn't work. I groped for my cell phone on the bedside table and turned on its flashlight. A layer of smoke hung near the bedroom ceiling. I threw on my robe, shoved my feet into my flip-flops and my wallet into my robe pocket. I hesitated at the door, laid a palm against the wood. Cool to the touch. I opened it slowly, heart pounding in my ears.

The flashlight bounced through a thick specter of smoke rolling across the living room ceiling. A nasty stench stung my nose. Plastic burning? Or rubber? Eyes watering, I looked toward the kitchen. Bright flames shot up the walls and over the cupboards. The curtains above the sink were ablaze.

The smoke ghost grew, fed by the flames devouring my home.

I stood, transfixed.

My parakeets' squawking snapped me back to the moment. Crouching below the smoke layer, I ran to Tweet and Chirp, wrapped my arms around the cage and bolted out the front door.

I ran across the street, where neighbors were gathering. Setting the birds down, I peeked under the cage cover. In the streetlight's glow, Tweet and Chirp huddled together on the bottom perch, shivering. "We're safe now," I told them. I heard sirens. "Help's coming."

"Mackenzie!" Mrs. Litowsky was already outside. She came over and threw her arms around me. "Oh, dear Gott! I saw you go out earlier, but I didn't hear you come home. You didn't tap! Dear Gott, dear Gott! If something had happened to you, I'd neffer forgive myself! Neffer!" Crying, she hugged me tighter.

"I'm so glad *you're* safe!" I said. Mrs. L watched out for me, but I hadn't given her safety a thought while I was saving my own hide. What kind of a person was I?

Two fire trucks rumbled up, and firefighters in bright yellow gear spilled out, hauling hoses from the first truck toward the back of the building. A fascinating dance of men and equipment, so smooth, so practiced. Efficient and comforting, and, if I stopped to think about it, the scariest thing ever.

An older firefighter approached our little group. "Who lives here?" he yelled over the cacophony. Mrs. Litowsky and I raised our hands obediently, like kids in school. "Anyone else in the building tonight?"

We both shook our heads. I added, "No, sir."

He glanced at the birdcage. "Any other pets inside?"

I leaned toward Mrs. Litowsky and hollered, "Where's Chloe?"

"She scooted out with me and ran for her life."

Assured that no other living beings—no cats, no boyfriends—were in our building, the firefighter explained that we would not be able to go back inside in the foreseeable future, until an assessment could be completed. The fire hadn't caused any damage to the buildings on either side of our duplex. Thank God.

I called my mother to let her know I was okay. Two of her friends had already called to tell her my building was on fire, and she yelled at me that she "had to hear it from those two busybodies before my own daughter."

"I'm sorry I didn't call you as soon as I smelled smoke," I shouted over the noise of the firetrucks, "but I was a little busy trying to avoid being burned alive!"

"Oh my God! Are you okay?"

"Just a little toasted around the edges," I said.

"Not funny. Not funny at all. I'll be right there," she said and disconnected.

Mrs. Litowsky called her sister, who lived a few blocks away; she'd stay with her sister and brother-in-law until things got squared away. A few minutes later, they picked Mrs. Litowsky up. She gave me another hug before she got in their car.

"Thank Gott you are safe," she said, petting my hair. "I'd neffer forgive myself, neffer, neffer . . ." She wiped away a tear as she released me, and I felt guilty again. I'd have to be extra nice to Mrs. L in the future, and buy Chloe a treat, if she ever came back. Cats and I don't usually get along, but Chloe is fiercely independent, never hesitating to make her wishes known, to go her own way. I admire that in a cat, and in people.

As Mrs. L and her family drove off, my grandmother arrived with my mother riding shotgun in Gram's "classic" maroon Buick Riviera. More a boat than an automobile, the car is my grandmother's pride and joy.

Gram had barely shoved it into park when she was out of the car, running toward me, my mother close behind. One on each side, they wrapped me in a hug.

Gram spoke first. "Mackenzie Annabelle Prentice! You scared the life out of us! My God, child, I'm so glad you're okay!" She stepped back and held me at arm's length, appraising. "You are okay, aren't you?"

"Yes, Gram. Nothing singed or scorched."

"Thank the good Lord!" Gram said. My mother still hadn't said a word. I looked at her. She stared at me, wide-eyed. She moved her mouth, but no sound came out. Finally, a little "oh" escaped, and she hugged me tight. I felt her shaking as she said, "I don't—" and "I can't—" before she started crying. Gram and I enveloped *her* in a hug.

When my mother finally pulled away, I turned to Gram. "I can't stay here. Okay if I stay with you?"

Gram gave me a look that said this was the most ridiculous question she'd ever heard. "Absolutely!" she said. "That big old house has room for you, the parakeets, and anyone else you know who needs a roof." With that, Gram turned to the small collection of neighbors who had come outside to watch the action. She cupped her hands around her mouth and yelled over the rumbles and hisses that filled the night. "Anyone else need a place to stay? We've got plenty of room!"

Nobody else took her up on her offer, so my mother, Gram, Tweet and Chirp, and I piled into the Buick and rolled back to Gram's.

CHAPTER TWENTY-FIVE

Monday, October 29

JUST AFTER TWO A.M., I leaned back into the pillows propped against the ornate metal headboard of the big bed in Gram's guest room. I'd had a quick shower and exchanged my smoke-infused attire for a pair of my mother's pajamas and one of Gram's chenille bathrobes.

Chirp and Tweet were quiet in their covered cage on the dresser, snug and safe. Nathan had slept through the whole thing.

I hadn't slept in this room since my early teens, the last of many sleepovers at Gram's. The earliest times here I shared this bed with my older sister, Stephanie. Serious and studious and six years my senior, Stephanie insisted we always go right to sleep, ignoring my pleas for stories.

After Stephanie went off to college, I shared this room with my little sister, Deanne, who is six years younger than I am. We'd whispered and shadow-puppeted half the night away in this bed. I'd tell her scary stories: how the fireplace in this bedroom, covered by an embossed metal panel, had been sealed up because the ghosts used it to come down from the attic.

She'd stare at me in the soft glow of the nightlight, enraptured. When I'd pause mid-sentence for dramatic effect, she'd whisper, "And *then* what?" My stories always had a happy ending, usually with the heroine, whose name was always Deanne, vanquishing the ghosts and saving the whole family.

Focusing on the memories instead of the trauma of the fire, I let my head relax into the pillow as my body settled deep into the cushy mattress. I pulled the soft pink sheet and quilt up to my chin.

Gram calls this the Rose Room because the walls are covered in rose-patterned wallpaper. The bedding is a coordinating pink, as is the area rug on the hardwood floor. Pink everywhere, which would be wonderful if I liked pink. Which I do not. But it's not my house.

And at the moment, you don't have a home, Rational Me said. *Be grateful.*

I let myself float down into the softness. The sheets smelled like fresh air and Gram. If I ignored the pinkness of it all, I could live happily ever after in this room.

I drifted back to other times I came to Gram's house as a kid after ice skating at Rawley Park. She and I would sit at the dining room table with our hot cocoa with marshmallows and buttered saltine crackers. She'd ask me about school, about my dreams, and she'd listen to the answers—things my mother, who was busy working at least two jobs to keep us kids clothed and fed, rarely had time for.

Gram has always been there for us. She smells like cookies and Dove soap. Her hugs hold decades of strength and love.

Her boundless energy belies her eighty years, and she is always on the move, taking care of the family, her home, her garden.

How does she do it all? She credits her Finnish heritage. "It's *sisu*," she says, that mysterious quality Finns claim. Some say it is courage, or stubbornness. Some say it is just willingness to do something challenging and to keep on, even in the face of overwhelming odds. However you translate it, Gram has it in spades.

At 2:35 a.m., after gagging down a glass of warm milk my mother gave me, which only became tolerable after Gram slipped a shot of brandy into it, I slept, lulled by the brandy and the comfort of the warmth from the cast-iron radiator and the tick-tocking of the grandfather clock on the staircase landing.

Old-fashioned comfort. Just what I needed.

CHAPTER TWENTY-SIX

MONDAY MORNING, I TOOK another extra-long, extra-hot shower, trying to clear the remaining stench of the fire from my nose. As I shampooed my hair a third time, I shuddered to think what could have happened if I'd not awakened. That dream, my brother Greg yelling, was like someone was watching out for me. Maybe someone was.

I'm not much for organized religion, but I do wonder if there is something out there—a higher power of some kind, maybe. Gram has faith. Raised in the Lutheran church, she's at Our Savior's pretty much every Sunday morning.

My mother grew up in church, too, and did her best to get us kids there on Sundays. It was probably hard enough for her, a single mother, to get the five of us out the door on school days. By the weekend, our mother was just pooped.

Where was our father? We don't know. He left one day and never returned. Once I grew up, my mother told me her side of the story. "Things just weren't working out, so we got divorced.

He moved to Sausalito, I think. Or maybe it was Saginaw. Or was it Syracuse? I don't know. It was S-something."

My grandmother's version? "Oh, he was a nasty piece of work. He left, and good riddance. He's probably in prison now. Or he should be." She's never offered more detail, even when I begged. "What does it matter anyway?" she said. "You all turned out great in spite of him."

So, depending on who you want to believe, my father is, or was, a nasty piece of work, a jailbird, and/or just a guy who left his wife and kids because he wanted to live in California. Or maybe Michigan. Or maybe New York. Regardless, I have only a dim memory of him. My younger brother and sister say they don't remember him at all.

Am I curious about all this? Of course. But finding answers? Beyond me. I wouldn't know where to start.

We kids spent a lot of time with Gram after my mother moved us here to Three Rivers. You could say she saved us, but she says, "Wasn't me! I prayed, and the Lord saved you all!" So maybe the someone watching out for me has been my praying grandmother.

All my deep thinking ended abruptly when the shower ran suddenly cold. Ah, yes. Gram's old water heater had trouble keeping up. I stepped out, dried off, dressed in a pair of my mother's sweatpants, a tee shirt from one of her races, and a sweatshirt with a huge red cardinal on the front—Gram's favorite bird. Socks from Gram, slippers from my mother. Outfit complete, I did what I could with my hair. I felt almost human again.

I met my mother in the hallway. She was dressed for her job at Lumber City Bank. "How are you feeling?" she asked.

"Better," I said. "I slept great in that bed."

"That old mattress is too soft. You'll end up with back trouble," she said. Always a negative with my mother. "I'm off to work. See you later." She trotted down the steps and out the front door, humming all the way.

I headed down to the kitchen. Gram grabbed me. "Are you okay, sweetie?"

Was I? Physically, yes. Unscorched. Mentally? Numb. Emotionally. Ditto. "I'm fine, really."

"Are you sure? Because I can stay home this morning if you need me." Gram meets with three of her friends for coffee and gossip every Monday morning at Hilda's Café on First Street.

"Absolutely not," I said. "You go have fun with the girls. I'll hang out here with Nathan."

After Gram left, I went up to their room to check on Nathan. He was still in bed, just waking up. I said, "Good morning, Nathan. How are you today?" He looked at me, brow furrowed.

"Where am I?"

"You're at home. Here."

"Where is here?"

"You live here with Gram. My grandmother."

He frowned, thinking. "No, I think my grandmother might be dead."

"No, not *your* grandmother. Mine. Remember Virginia?"

"I don't think I've ever been to Virginia, have I?"

"Not the state. The person. My grandmother. Your wife."

"I've got a wife?"

"Yes."

"For how long?"

"Well, you've been married for several years." I wasn't quite sure how many.

"No, I mean, how long before she bails out on me. I mean,

I'm losing my marbles, and no sensible woman is going to want to stick around to see how that ends." He smiled and winked at me.

I laughed. "Good morning, Nathan. Nice to have you back."

"Good to be here! Good to be anywhere! What's for breakfast?"

I left him to get dressed and went downstairs to whip up eggs and toast for the two of us. Two eggs scrambled in butter. "The fat is good for his brain," Gram says. Two pieces of toast with more butter, and strawberry preserves. "Not the jelly. Preserves. Got to have some fiber," Gram says.

And coffee, also good for us, Gram says. With a splash of cream. "Not the fat-free fake stuff, but real whipping cream. Fat is good for the brain," Gram repeats. Since Gram is incredibly sharp, nobody wants to argue about what she eats.

I needed to start adding whipping cream to my coffee.

Ten minutes later, Nathan appeared in the kitchen doorway. "Well, Mackenzie! Nice of you to stop by."

I looked hard at him, trying to determine if he was kidding. He walked to the table and sat down at his place. "When did you get here? Where's Virginia?"

"On the east coast?" I said.

"Huh?" He looked puzzled.

"I'm sorry, Nathan. That was a feeble joke. Virginia went to her coffee group. She'll be back in a bit."

"Oh, good. I thought maybe today we could go out to the farm." Nathan and his brother Clark grew up on a farm in Illinois, but it had been sold years ago. He'd forgotten. Very sad. But Gram had taught us all to just go with the flow with Nathan's memory.

"Sure. It looks like it might be a nice day for a drive, Nathan."

He looked at me. "A drive? Where are we going?"

"To the farm?"

"The farm? No can do. My brother and I sold off that old place years ago. Pass the strawberry jam, please, Mackenzie?"

And he was back. Keeping up with Nathan can be exhausting.

CHAPTER TWENTY-SEVEN

N ATHAN FINISHED HIS BREAKFAST and went into the family room to watch *The Price Is Right*. I poured another cup of coffee from Gram's old electric percolator and sat down to read the morning paper—the *Three Rivers Bulletin*, aka *The Bull*. Like so many newspapers these days, this one is getting smaller and smaller, as advertisers have increasing access to customers online. *The Bull* has done a decent job building an online presence, but folks like Gram prefer the hard copy, home delivered.

I tried to read the paper but calls from my siblings interrupted every third paragraph. Stephanie called first. My mother had texted her earlier. Deanne called a few minutes later; my mother had caught her taking the four-year-old twins and their two-year-old brother to daycare. Deanne is very pregnant with child number four and sounded out of breath. But then again, Deanne always sounds out of breath.

My younger brother Robbie texted from LA. "Glad you're okay. Talk later?" He lives a successful-single-guy-in-LA kind of life; with the two-hour time difference, I was surprised he was awake. I shot him a smiley emoji. He texted back a thumbs-up.

Brother Greg called. Our mother had called him, but his firefighter friend Vince, who had been at the fire, had beat her to it.

After making sure I was okay, he said, "Expect a call from Vince. He's the investigator for the department. You remember?"

Oh, I remembered Vince. He'd been my primary torturer in middle school, calling me "Macaroni Annabelly. Smack-aroni Banana-belly."

I told Greg about my dream, and he agreed it was freaky. "'There are more things in heaven and earth,'" he said, then stopped and cleared his throat. "Just listen to me, gettin' all philosophical. I'm just glad you got out of there."

"Me too. Thanks for saving me, brother."

He got quiet, then said, his voice soft, "Anytime." He took a breath. "Okay, gotta go."

I started to say, "Love you," but he was gone.

I'd just settled back in to read when Vince called. After pleasantries, he launched into official business. "We don't know the cause yet," he said, "so we can't rule anything out. Could be a wiring issue, appliance malfunction, arson—"

"Arson?" A chill chased up my spine. "What are you saying? Who would do that?" I felt panic rising.

"Whoa!" Vince said. "I'm just saying we have to check all the possibilities." I swallowed hard as Vince went on.

"We won't know for sure until we've finished investigating. There's extensive fire and water damage to the back half of the building. And now that the walls and ceilings are opened, there may be an asbestos issue. If that's the case, the owner will have to bring in an abatement team. The place will need major reconstruction before it's habitable again."

This was not good. I couldn't imagine my cheapo landlord paying for major renovations.

Vince must have read my mind. "Your landlord told me he's not sure if he wants to fix the place or tear it all down and start over. Sorry I don't have better news, but I'd suggest you make alternate living arrangements."

"For how long?" I asked.

"Maybe weeks, months. Maybe forever."

Asbestos. Damage. Extensive. Arson. Scary, powerful words. The fire was so much worse than I'd thought. I saw the flames, smelled the smoke again. Panic rose. My throat tightened. *Breathe, breathe, breathe . . .*

Vince must have heard my deep breathing. "Are you okay, Mackenzie?"

I blew out a long breath. "Yeah, just a little freaked out." I inhaled, willing myself to calm. "So, what about my clothes, my laptop?" Gram and my mother were sharing, but I missed the familiarity—the comfort—of my *own* stuff.

"Don't know what all survived the fire. But you'll be able to retrieve personal property, with an escort and a hazmat suit, once we know what we're dealing with. I'll let you know. And one more thing. Who owns the green Chevy that was parked behind the building?"

Charlotte. I hadn't given her a thought. "That's my car," I squeaked.

"You can pick it up anytime. Might have some blistering in the paint from the heat, but it should still run. Just be careful where you step, and don't go near the structure."

I glanced toward the wooden key rack by Gram's back door. Spare keys for my car and my apartment hung there. I'd given the keys to my mother in the past, "just in case." Maybe I was more like her than I wanted to admit.

I thanked Vince for calling and was ready to hang up when he said, "Greg told me about your ex. Sorry to hear that." I thanked him again. He continued, "I was wondering if maybe—once things settle down for you—if maybe you'd like to go out for a drink or something sometime."

Hmmm. Despite his teasing, I'd always had a bit of a little-sister crush on big brother's friend Vince. I'd heard that Vince had gotten divorced. And Frank and I had just had the one date. Not like I owed Frank anything.

I smiled into the phone. "Sure, Vince."

I could hear the smile in his voice. "Great. Okay. Take care, Anna—er, Mackenzie," he said and disconnected.

As the call ended, Gram came back from her coffee group. She and Nathan sat at the kitchen table. My mother came in the back door. I looked at the clock. Almost noon.

"Home so soon?"

"Half day today. I'll make lunch. Who wants a sandwich? Turkey and cheese?"

Gram and I declined, but Nathan accepted her offer.

I said, "Mom, I've heard from everyone. When the heck did you have time to make all those calls?"

She turned her head and scowled at me over her shoulder, then turned back to slicing cheese. "Well, I couldn't sleep at all. That was just so upsetting last night. I made some calls. Sorry if that bothers you, but I knew they'd want to know. We're family!"

I felt myself bristling but then took another breath. My mother could be annoying, but she meant well. Most of the time. I walked over and hugged her from behind. "Thanks, Mom."

She patted my arm. "I'm just glad you're okay," she said.

I sat back down at the table and related what Vince had said about the fire.

Gram clapped her hands. "That's wonderful!"

I frowned. "What are you talking about? This is not wonderful. It's horrible!"

"I just mean you don't have to move back into that awful apartment. You can stay right here with us!"

My apartment was not awful; it was my home. I started to defend the old place but stopped. Gram's idea wasn't bad. I'd be close enough to help if Gram needed me. And with Nathan, she needed more help every day.

But living under the same roof as my mother? That was another story.

Gram continued. "You can stay here in the house for now while we fix up the carriage house. Then you'd have your own place but still be close. That carriage house could be adorable fixed up."

"I had a carriage once," Nathan said.

"Yes, dear," Gram said and reached over to pat his arm.

I said, "I could help pay for the renovations—" and caught myself before I blurted out anything about the money from Billy. I finished with, "once I get a job."

"I had a job once," Nathan said.

Gram took his hand in hers and patted it, then turned to me. "No, you will *not* pay for the renovation. I've been wanting to do something back there for years." She winked and said, "Let's just say Chester and The Hussy will be funding this project."

I smiled. Nathan opened his mouth to say something—maybe "I knew a hussy once"—but then closed it again and focused on his coffee instead.

After Nathan finished his sandwich, he and Gram went upstairs. As my mother and I cleaned up the kitchen, Mom said, "I don't know how my mother puts up with him."

I frowned. "Nathan's not a bad guy, just forgetful."

"She's been widowed twice, and now this. When does she get to be happy? When does she get to enjoy her life? She's spent her life taking care of everybody else, and now she's *his* caretaker."

"I think we're supposed to say care*giving*, not care*taking*," I said.

"Semantics. It's taking. *Life* taking. Her life. I hate to see her with this burden. When does she get a break?"

"She doesn't seem to mind," I said.

"Oh, for God's sake, Mackenzie. Open your eyes. We women take care of everybody all our lives, and in the end, what do you see? Single women. Divorced, widowed, single older women. Where are the men? All gone. Dead. We start out alone; we end up alone. That's just how it works."

I had a feeling she wasn't talking about Gram anymore. "Geez, Mom. Is it really that bad? Don't you think about finding someone yourself?"

"Why start something that will just end in heartbreak? It's a cruel trick, really. God wires us for relationship. We want it. We need it. But we just get our hearts broken. It's cruel. And just not fair."

We finished the cleanup in silence. I hated to think life was that miserable. I wanted to think that I could find my own happily ever after someday. Someday soon, preferably. But there seemed to be a lot of not-so-happy endings for a lot of the women I knew—and for me, too, lately. Billy. Kyle. My job. My apartment.

My mother tended to be cynical and negative, but maybe she had a point. We're not in charge. Maybe God, the universe, or whatever is playing cruel tricks on us. Or maybe we're the ones who screw things up. Who knows? Not me, that's for sure.

Kyle texted later that day asking about his sweatshirt again. I texted back, Kyle-style: "DK. HD APT FIR." Let him figure it out.

A minute later, he replied, using some full words this time. Impressive. "Fire? OMG. When can I gt swtsht?"

Seriously, Kyle? I could have died, and all you care about is your stupid shirt? The guy had the compassion of a gnat. I felt sorry for the poor people of Bangladesh.

Angry Me felt a little white flame of fury in my chest— angry at Kyle, angry at the fire. I thought about telling him I'd burned his stupid shirt myself. But Rational Me texted that I had to wait before I could get back in there to see if it survived.

"OK," he texted. That's it.

Geez! What had I ever seen in that jerk?

CHAPTER TWENTY-EIGHT

I T'S A SHOCK TO be suddenly homeless, to lose everything you own—or in my case, not actually knowing what I'd lost. And not knowing what survived the fire was driving me crazy.

Gram came back downstairs after tucking Nathan in for a nap. I told her I needed to go get my car, so she drove, parking in the alley behind the building. My heart raced, and my throat felt tight as I looked at the place. Gram averted her eyes. "I can't look," she said. "Too hard to see it, to think about . . ."

I didn't want to cause Gram more distress. She waited while I started Charlotte. After I gave her a thumbs up, she sped off down the alley.

I checked Charlotte over. She was intact. I opened her trunk; Bob was there, packed full of my essentials, including jeans, running shoes, and a couple of tee shirts. I sighed in relief. *Hallelujah! And thank you, my anxious mother!*

I left Charlotte running while I walked around the building. I wanted to look in the windows. I wanted to see for myself.

The drapes on my front windows were closed but still there. I took that as a good sign. In fact, from the front, there was no indication of the fire other than a yellow CAUTION—DO NOT ENTER tape strung across the door. I walked to the side of the building, checking my bedroom window. Drapes closed and intact.

I returned to the back. Charlotte was still running; I reached in and turned off the ignition since I couldn't remember when I'd last filled the tank, and her gas gauge wasn't trustworthy. Wasn't my gas tank supposed to explode when the building was on fire? That's what would have happened in the movies. But this was real life, not some movie script, thank God. Or whoever. Or whatever.

I looked at the small back porch, where Mrs. Litowsky had stood asking me if I needed anything from the store. Seemed like ages ago, not just yesterday. Burnt wood slats that had once formed the porch roof lay on what was left of the porch floor, now a mass of splintered, charred boards.

Broken glass shards—from my kitchen window and the glass in the back door—littered the porch and steps. I didn't see anywhere safe to step. Somebody—my landlord or someone he hired—had covered the window over the kitchen sink and the back door with plywood and another caution tape.

Looking up, I saw where the flames had blistered and blackened the siding all the way up to the roof. I shivered, remembering the flames in my kitchen, the rolling smoke, the acrid smell. What was that? Melting plastic? Burning rubber? What did asbestos smell like when it burned?

Above my window, Mrs. Litowsky's kitchen window was unbroken, her philodendron still hanging above her sink. Weird how one thing is ruined, and right next to it, another thing is unscathed. Like when a tornado leaves one house demolished and the next one untouched.

I went to my side kitchen window, which had not been broken, and stood on tiptoe to peek inside. Cans and boxes littered the floor and what was left of the cupboards. Cereal. My Toasty-Os were, indeed, toasty. Mac and cheese, now black and charred. *Bummer.* Seeing them, I felt sick and a little hungry at the same time.

A melted lump sat on the counter where I'd left the loaf of whole wheat bread Mrs. Litowsky brought me from the store. She'd been so concerned about my fiber. The least of my worries. The drawer where I kept my cash was blackened. How much money was in there? Twenty bucks or so, probably incinerated.

I headed toward my car, turning to look at the building once more. Maybe the fire wasn't that bad; maybe only the porch and my kitchen were affected. Maybe I'd be back in my apartment sooner than Vince thought. Maybe there wasn't any asbestos. Maybe my cheap landlord would rebuild my apartment better than ever.

As Gram says, "Wishing doesn't make it so."

Had Chloe tried to come home? I pictured her poor little paws walking through the shattered glass, ashes, and splinters covering the ground back here. She wasn't such a bad cat. I hoped she was okay.

"What caused this?" I asked nobody. Vince said it could have been an electrical problem. Or was it arson? Why? Because I'd been asking questions about Billy's death? I shivered again.

I looked around for signs of a Molotov cocktail. I'd seen that kind of thing on TV. The glass on the ground was just window glass, as far as I could tell. No broken beer bottles with telltale rags sticking out of the tops.

Snarky Me spoke up. *Duh. Wouldn't that have ended up inside the place, not outside?*

Rational Me weighed in. *This is why we have trained arson investigators like Vince. Regular people are absolutely clueless about these things. Let the professionals figure it out.*

Giving the building one last look, I was ready to leave when someone behind me yelled, "Hey!" Before I could turn around, someone body-slammed me from behind. I let out an "Ugh!" as I stumbled forward, tripping over the debris on the ground and face-planting—hard—into what was left of the porch steps.

My face met burnt and broken wood, sending a shock of pain through my right cheek. I groaned and pressed up to hands and knees, pushing my left hand into broken glass. I yelped and scrambled to stand.

I turned. Someone ran away down the alley. Hoodie Guy, I was positive. I screamed, "What the hell?" Hoodie looked back for just a fraction of a second. I squinted in the bright sunlight, saw a glint of something, but couldn't make out his face. Then he was gone.

I felt a throb of pain in my left hand. Blood oozed from a chunk of glass protruding from my palm. I grabbed it with my right thumb and index finger and tugged it out. *Ooh, crap!* Blood spurted from the hole. I pressed it against the leg of my borrowed pants. I touched my face, near my right eye. Warm blood oozed down my cheek. The cut on my face was close to my eye and probably full of burnt splinters. *Son of a...!* I blinked back tears.

As I limped toward Charlotte, my knees protested. I looked down. The pants were torn, exposing my kneecaps, both embedded with gravel and glass.

I wanted to scream, so I did. "Yeoww!"

I wanted to swear, so I did. "Damn! Damn! Damn it!"

I wanted revenge, to jump in my car, race down the alley, and introduce Hoodie Guy's rear end to Charlotte's front end. But I didn't. Instead, I started to cry. I whimpered to nobody, "I want my mommy."

I drove back to Gram's one-handed, which is a lot harder than you'd think. I used my left hand to press a wad of tissues I found in my car against the right side of my face. This stemmed the tide of blood from both palm and cheek.

Back at the house, my mother and grandmother took one look at me and went into full-on Doctor Mom mode. As I told them what happened, they spoke in their softest you'll-be-fine-sweetie voices as they applied disinfectant to my hand, pulled splinters from my face, and picked gravel from my knees. All the while, they discussed whether I needed stitches and should be checked for a concussion.

I stepped away from their fussing to limp to the bathroom mirror. My face, red and swollen around my right eye, ached. The cut didn't seem too deep, but since it was on my face, I let them take me to the ER.

I rode in the back seat, pressing a cloth wrapped around a bag of frozen peas to my cheek as Gram drove and my mother rode shotgun. I closed my eyes, and Gram must have noticed in the rearview mirror. She turned toward me and yelled, "Stay awake, Mackenzie!"

The car swerved toward the wrong side of the road. She brought the Buick back onto our side of the street and then turned toward my mother. "Barbara, make sure she stays awake! Velma's nephew's son had a concussion from playing football, and they said if he went to sleep, his brain could explode." We almost hit a parked car before Gram got us back on track.

My mom yelled, "Mother! Keep your eyes on the road, or

you'll get us all killed!" Maybe they'd really get into it. That would be way more entertaining than anything on Netflix.

In the ER, a nurse named Darren numbed my face, cleaned the wound, and closed it with tape. He assured me the cut was shallow and I'd heal in no time. My left hand would be fine, too, the cut now closed with two stitches, which he said would dissolve on their own. Gram and my mom had done a good job cleaning my knees.

"No major issues," he said. Easy for Darren to say. I felt as if I'd been hit by a truck. After a tetanus shot, since I couldn't remember when I got the last one, I dozed off and on, waiting to be discharged.

"Where is that doctor? We need to get going," my mother said.

As if by magic, a guy appeared from behind the curtain. Gorgeous, he had a golfer's tan, just the right amount of gray at his temples, and an athletic build evident even under the lab coat. He smiled at me, and I swear I saw one of those stars twinkle off a tooth. That might have been the painkiller they'd given me. I smiled back, but it may have been more of a wince.

"Let's see how we are," he said as he leaned in to inspect my face, shining a light in my eyes. His breath smelled like cake. "Mmm-hmmm," he said. "Looks good." He straightened up and continued. "No evidence of concussion. You may have a headache; take Tylenol if you need it." He summarized the symptoms of concussion and infection. "If you don't have any questions, you can get out of here."

"Is it okay if I go to sleep when I get home?" I asked. I felt bone-weary and wanted the doctor to tell my grandmother it was okay.

"Yes, you should rest," he said, then turned to Mom and Gram. "I assume she'll have care at home. Right?" They both nodded wordlessly. Nothing like an authority figure to shut those two up.

He left, and Gram fanned herself with her hands. "Whew! Doctors never used to be that good-looking!"

My mom rolled her eyes. "Oh, for the love of God! Mother!"

"Hey! I'm old, not dead!" Gram said. "Maybe he's single. I didn't see a ring. Maybe you could hook up."

I giggled. My mom shot us both a dirty look. "Shut up, both of you!"

My head hurt, and I felt woozy. I closed my eyes. My mind played back the scene at the apartment, but it was like looking through fog. The blistered siding, the stench, the burnt wood, the shards of glass. The cut, the blood, the splinters. What had happened, exactly?

Suddenly the fog cleared, and the scene ran in slow motion. I heard, "Hey!" Felt the push, felt myself falling, pushing back up. Pain. Blood. Saw him running away into the sun, all in slo-mo. There was something there, something I'd seen or heard, just beyond my awareness. I pressed my eyes closed harder, trying to concentrate, trying to remember, but nothing.

I came back to the present as Gram shook me. "Look at me! Open your eyes and look at me!" she ordered, then got close to my face, staring into my eyes. I stared back. "Velma told me her nephew's son's concussion made his eyeballs all wonky, like his eyes were two different sizes all of a sudden. Yours look okay, but I want to keep checking."

"Are you gonna keep waking me up, Gram? I'm really tired."

"I'll wake you up every five minutes if I have to! You could have died!"

I smiled and closed my eyes again. When Gram is around, you can't help feeling loved. And annoyed.

CHAPTER TWENTY-NINE

LATER THAT AFTERNOON, AFTER I'd had a nap, I found Gram folding laundry on the couch in front of the TV as she watched a *Little House on the Prairie* rerun. She loves that channel that plays all the old family fare, those shows with no sex or violence, with characters like Andy of Mayberry and John-Boy Walton, always being kind and sensible. And where every problem of life is solved in less than an hour. If only life were like that.

I sat down on the other side of the laundry pile and started folding towels. Gram frowned at me, checked my eyeballs again. "No wonkiness. But you should be resting. How's your headache?"

I assured her I felt fine. No headache, no nausea. Just a little sore around the cheek, but otherwise, okay. I changed the subject. "So, how are things at the *Little House?*"

Gram chuckled. "Oh, that Nellie. She sure keeps things interesting, doesn't she?" I agreed.

Gram held up a pair of her underpants. "Look at these things! What do people call them now? Granny panties?"

I laughed. "I guess those qualify."

Gram chuckled. "My mother would call them *dainties*, but there's nothing dainty about them. There's plenty of material here to cover your bottom and then some. I don't know how any girl could feel comfortable in those whatchamacallits that leave your backside bare."

"Thongs?"

"Yes! Thongs. Who in heaven's name invented those? Who could ever relax wearing something like that? And I heard some women get tattoos or even piercings down there. Or they wax everything. Oh Lordy! That's gotta be painful!" Gram winced. "I figure, if the good Lord put it there, I'm gonna leave it there!" She stood to fold a sheet. "Grab the other end of this, will you?"

I stood, and as Gram brought her two corners together, I did the same. Then we stepped forward to join our ends. When Gram was close to my face, she whispered, "Don't tell your mother, but I'm thinking about getting a tattoo."

I choked back a laugh. We stepped back, brought our corners together again, and when Gram stepped close, I whispered, "Your secret's safe with me, Nellie."

Yep. Gram keeps things interesting.

As we finished folding clothes, I filled her in on what I'd seen at the apartment. "It looked like the fire was just in the back end of the building. I didn't see anything suspicious, but what do I know? Vince will be able to tell if it was arson."

Gram sucked in a breath. "Arson? Seriously? Someone set that fire on purpose?"

I didn't want to worry her, so I didn't tell her about Hoodie-Stalker. I didn't tell Gram that I'd been playing detective, snooping around, trying to figure out what really happened to Billy, and somebody didn't like that.

Instead, I said, "Nah. It was probably a short or something."

She frowned again, staring at me for a long moment. Then her face softened. "I know it's hard, honey, but I'm glad you're going to be living here with us. I worried about you in that old place."

"Thanks for taking me in, but I should be supporting myself, making my own way in life." And I had been until I got canned by Trip. And the fire. "So, I'll just be here a little while—until I can get back to my apartment. It won't be long. And I'll pay rent."

Gram's voice took on a my-mind-is-made-up tone. "Not to me, you won't. Besides, working part-time for Lou isn't going to cover much. And it's silly to worry about staying too long when we've got enough room for ten more people in this house. I won't hear another word about it. That room upstairs is *your* room, and the carriage house can be yours down the road if you want it. There. Settled. Done."

Gram was exaggerating a little; the house might hold a few more people, but probably not ten. But she was missing the point. A person my age should be able to support herself, pay rent and her bills without relying on anyone, right? *Right?*

I said, "Right!" out loud.

Gram smiled. "I'm glad you agree, dear."

I started to say, "But I didn't mean—" and then stopped. No point in arguing with Gram once her mind is made up. And why argue, really? Gram's house is warm and holds an endless supply of cookies. And there was that soft, soft bed upstairs. And the sweet memories.

Maybe it was okay to let someone else take care of me for the time being, even though, as my mother had said, Gram was already burdened with taking care of Nathan. But then again, I had just been through a pretty traumatic experience myself.

Gram went on, reading my mind. Again. "You know, dear, you've just been through a scary experience." She furrowed her brow and looked at me more closely. "You probably have that PSPD thing."

"PSPD?" I paused. "I think PSPD stands for the Palm Springs Police Department," I teased.

"Oh, pish-tush. You know what I mean."

"Well, I can't read your mind like you seem to be able to read mine, but I'm guessing you mean PTSD?"

"Yes! That's what Nathan's brother Wallace had after the war. He was real depressed and then got really paranoid as he got older, Nathan said. Kept thinking he was under attack. Wouldn't even come out of his house." The brow furrow got deeper. "You don't think that will happen to you, do you? I don't mind you staying here temporarily, but you really do need to get out of the house."

"Not to worry, Gram. I love you, but being in the house with Mom will keep me from getting too settled here."

"Okay, that's good," Gram said. "I'd hate for you to go off the deep end."

What I didn't say at that point was that if I were going to go off the deep end, it would not be because of the fire but because I spent too much time with my mother.

As if reading my mind again, she said, "I know how it is with mothers and daughters." She let out a deep sigh. "I don't know where your mother got all that anxiety. Maybe I was a bad mom. You know, with the six kids and no money, things were pretty tense for your Papa and me at times."

"Maybe my mom is just wired that way," I said. "It's nobody's fault, really." Gram had done a Herculean job as a mother, and I didn't for a moment want her to take any blame for how any of her children, or grandchildren, turned out.

"Maybe so, but mothers always feel guilty," she said. I felt sad that Gram felt that way, and hearing her say it made me more sure than ever that I never wanted to be a mother.

I'd watched my sister Deanne and Greg's wife, Sarah, struggling with their feelings of "mommy guilt." Was this kid getting enough vitamin C? Was that one scarred for life because his mother yelled at him? They seemed to feel guilty for doing too much and for doing too little, for being too protective and not being protective enough. They couldn't seem to win.

They always seemed to be wrangling a child or two or, for Greg's wife, three. And for Deanne, soon to be four. "Enjoy your freedom while you've got it," Deanne said to me one day when the family had gathered for our mother's birthday. She bounced a toddler on her hip as she said, "Because once these little buggers come along, your carefree days are done."

Sarah chimed in. "Yup. And you can kiss that body goodbye." They laughed together then as if they were in a secret club to which I did not belong, but they seemed certain that one day I would. I did not share that certainty. In fact, every time they made these jokes, I became firmer in my resolve. Nope. No kids for me. Not ever.

Why were these kinds of comments always directed toward the women in the family? Nobody ever said such things to my brother Robbie, who was as single as I was. Nobody ever warned him that he would lose his freedom if he became a father. And, of course, if that day ever came, it would be the woman in his life who would "kiss that body goodbye." She'd have the stretch marks. She'd carry the mom guilt. Is there even such a thing as "dad guilt?"

Maybe my mother was right. Maybe life was simply not fair.

CHAPTER THIRTY

I SAT THAT EVENING AT the dining room table with Gram, Nathan, and my mother, trying and failing to enjoy roast beef, mashed potatoes, gravy, and Gram's melt-in-your-mouth biscuits. This was real comfort food, and I certainly needed some comfort as the trauma of the fire and the assault sank in.

What-ifs swirled in my mind. What if I hadn't awakened? What if Mrs. Litowsky had been trapped upstairs? Dark imaginings. I'd tried to nap, but every time I closed my eyes, I heard the smoke alarm screaming and something else churning in the undercurrent of my thoughts. What was it? A sound? A smell? I couldn't quite grasp it, but it was right there, just beyond my awareness. I reviewed my dream. The hallway of my childhood home, Greg calling, following him, losing him in the smoke.

Gram's voice broke in. "My friend Velma has a theory about how your Billy died. She says he was probably working for the CIA, and one of those drug cartel guys killed him because he was threatening their operation."

My mom laughed. "Oh, Mother, for heaven's sake. You saw that on TV the other night."

Gram laughed. "Did I? Huh. Everything kind of runs together these days."

"I don't know that there is a lot of drug cartel action in Deerwood," I said.

My mother said, "Well, my friend Ellen has a theory too. That Billy loved you so much that he just died of a broken heart." Ellen is in my mother's knitting group of several women who meet once a month to knit together. Ellen could knit anything from sweaters to socks. My mother just keeps making winter scarves, insisting, "People can always use another scarf." (My collection of scarves stands at fifteen. Thanks, Mom.)

I cringed. "Not likely. Billy demonstrated pretty clearly in the last few months of our marriage that he was spreading his love around. More likely, his latest girlfriend broke his heart."

Gram piped up. "I think it was the cartel guy. I vote for him."

My mother sighed. "This isn't an election. Or *America's Got Talent*."

Gram said, "All the girls in the coffee klatsch like that idea." So, Gram's group and Mom's friends all had theories about Billy's death. What was mine? He overdosed, yes, but accidentally or on purpose? Or someone staged it because he may have discovered something someone didn't want him to know. Or he may have eaten some bad chicken, which was highly probable, given what I'd found in the cabin refrigerator.

But for all my nosing around, I wasn't any closer to being sure than when I started. Maybe I wasn't so great at figuring things out.

Gram's landline rang, and I got up to answer it. Gram doesn't have caller ID. (I'd asked her why not. She said, "I like surprises." I warned her, "Just wait until you get an obscene call." She smiled. "Like I said, I like surprises.")

"Hello?" Silence. I repeated, "Hello?" No response, just breathing. *Good grief. An obscene phone call? Seriously?* I listened for another few seconds. "Hell-OH! Who is this?" No response, then a click. I star-sixty-nined. Blocked number.

Gram called from the dining room. "Who is it, Mackenzie?"

I hung up and went back to the table. "They didn't say."

Gram said, "I'll bet it was the cartel guy. Ooh. He knows where we live now. Maybe he's coming here next."

I shook my head. "Seriously, Gram? Why would he do that?"

"Because whatever it was that got Billy killed, the cartel guy figures you know it, and they are coming after you next! How thrilling!" She paused and then frowned. "Maybe we should get a gun."

My mother spoke up. "Mother! You're saying it's thrilling that my daughter could be killed? And now you want a gun? What is wrong with you?"

Gram winked at me and then turned to my mother. "And, Barbara, you might want to sleep with one eye open too. You never know with those cartel guys."

My mother gave a grunt of disgust. "Ugh. That's enough for me!" She said she'd see us later and left the room.

Gram turned serious. "Mackenzie, I'm truly sorry that Billy is gone. I know you cared about him. This must be awful for you. I didn't mean to make light of it all." She reached forward and squeezed my hand.

"Thanks, Gram. But Billy and I were over a long time ago. I just want to know what really happened to him."

"So not the cartel, then?"

"Not likely in Deerwood," I said.

"A jealous husband, maybe?"

"Not that I can tell, but I guess that's another possibility."

I told her what I knew so far and showed her the key. She fingered it. "Sounds like this key is the key." She chuckled and then said, "This looks like the kind of key you'd use to wind a mantel clock. Didn't you have one of those?"

I almost gave myself a forehead smack. *Duh*. Of course. This was the key for the ugly clock we had, not a mailbox, a post office box, or any other box somewhere. But where was it now? Not in the cabin. And what was so important about it that Billy made sure I got this key? *Geez, Billy, why couldn't you just leave a frickin' note saying, 'Hey Mack, here's the key to that ugly old clock we had, and the clock is . . .' Where, Billy?*

CHAPTER THIRTY-ONE

Tuesday, October 30

B Y TUESDAY AFTERNOON, MY eye had a lovely purple and green aura around it. The swelling in my face had gone down, but my cheek was still tender to the touch. I told the girl in the mirror, "You look fierce!" She told me, "I'm a badass!" I agreed.

I found Gram in the back parlor of the Victorian, which we call the family room. A yoga DVD played on the TV. Gram had her backside up in the air, hands on the floor in front of her. Down Dog. She looked at me from between her knees and laughed. "Oh, dear! Not my best side!" She stood up, grabbed the remote, and paused the DVD player.

Gram looked darned good in her pink leotard, pink tights, and pink and white striped leg warmers. The woman does love pink.

"Like the outfit?" she asked. I nodded. "Picked it up at Lou's." Lou's Vintage was Gram's go-to store for second-hand goodies. She bought dishes and bric-a-brac there, sharing her treasures with anyone who would listen to her long explanations of when she used to have this or that, or her memories of her own mother or grandmother having one thing or another. I braced myself for the story about her current outfit.

"I remember back in the old days, watching Jane Fonda do her aerobics. It was on the VCR back then. Remember those? I'll bet Lou has some of those old machines in her back room." I nodded again as I sat on the couch; this was going to take a while.

Gram went on. "I felt like I was in Jane's little class there in her aerobics studio. She invented aerobics, you know. I admired her outfits, so when I saw this at Lou's, well . . ." Gram smiled and twirled around, modeling.

"You look great, Gram, just like Jane!"

"Well, I'll never be one to protest a war like she did during Vietnam. That was not Jane's finest hour, not when all our boys were dying over there. But I don't think it's fair to hold one youthful mistake against someone for the rest of her life." She paused and then brightened. "She made up for it by giving us aerobics."

"And leg warmers," I added.

Gram smiled. "Yes, aerobics and leg warmers changed the world! Care to join me?" She turned back to the TV and pressed play. I stood and bent at the waist as she resumed the downward dog position. "You know, Jane and I are pretty much the same age," Gram said. "But she looks younger. Those Hollywood people spend a fortune to keep from getting wrinkles!"

"You don't need that. You're gorgeous."

"And it doesn't cost me a cent!" The instructor had us stretching into what she called Lizard Pose. I heard Gram's hip pop as she grunted. Then she said, "Oh, by the way, the mystery is solved."

"What mystery?" My hip was starting to hurt. The TV told us to shift back to Table Top, just in time.

Gram went on. "That mystery phone message. Remember? The one I erased by accident? It kept bugging me, and I worried that you might be in some kind of danger. So, at coffee, I told the girls about it, and Velma turned all red and said, 'Oh, I'm so sorry, Ginny. That was me!'"

"Velma? What the heck?"

Gram said, as we shifted into second side Lizard, "I asked why the heck she was disguising her voice, and she said she wasn't. She had a little laryngitis and then got a coughing spell and hung up."

I was confused. "I don't get why she called in the first place. What did she mean about leaving something alone? *Who* is supposed to leave *what* alone?"

Gram laughed. "Velma thought she'd called her sister. She's got one of those fancy phones with the speed dialing thingy." *Fancy for its time, indeed. Back in the Stone Age.* "They'd just had a big fight, and her sister was going on and on about it with everyone else in the family and even on Facebook. And Velma just wanted her to shut up. Velma said she was steaming mad, and her hearing isn't that great. Maybe it's all that banging around with the Snow Shovel Brigade."

We grunted into Warrior Two as Gram continued. "Velma didn't even listen to the greeting, just started talking, so all we heard was the end of the thing before she started coughing. Good grief. Who can't handle an answering machine? I told her, 'For gosh sakes, get with the twenty-first century, Velma!'"

I chuckled at the irony as we yoga-ed on. A few moves later, Gram groaned as she tried to follow the instruction to place her left foot in a particular spot. She yelled at the TV screen, "I'm *sorry*, Missy, but that part just doesn't belong there!"

Something clicked in my brain. It wasn't exactly like that moment in *Murder She Wrote* where Jessica Fletcher suddenly figures things out. Or the moment when Hercule Poirot's "little gray cells" have worked their magic. I wasn't ready to gather all the suspects, like Miss Marple, and point to the murderer with, "You dunnit!" This wasn't a work of fiction but real life. I didn't have all the answers, but I did know what I needed to do next.

"Gotta go, Gram," I said, hugging her as she bent forward.

"Okay, Sweetie. See you later—if I survive." She laughed, groaned, and laughed again. I left her laughing and headed for the most likely place that old clock would be.

Cabin. Crawl space. Guarded by a skunk.

CHAPTER THIRTY-TWO

CHARLOTTE AND I HEADED north after two o'clock that afternoon. My left palm hurt; I favored my right hand on the drive. It had been a week since the funeral. The early afternoon had turned chilly. Maybe the endless summer would end after all. I'd borrowed a sweater from my mother's closet to wear with the jeans and hiking boots I'd retrieved from my car.

Before I left, I made sure Tweet and Chirp had fresh water and plenty of the seed my mother picked up on her grocery run. The birdseed at my apartment was probably toasted, just part of the post-inferno hazmat disaster. Gram had insisted I move the birdcage from the dresser in the Rose Room to the dining room, near the big bay window, "so they can see their bird friends outside," she said.

I planned to go straight to the cabin, hoping to find what I hoped I'd find. Then I'd decide my next steps. I left Ben Marks a voicemail, letting him know where I was going and that I'd call later to connect. With luck, I'd be back home before bedtime.

Halfway to Deerwood, Frank called. I pulled to the shoulder.

"Hey, Mackenzie, great news! Miss Taylor is back," he said. The rumor about her connecting with a guy online proved to be true. She'd gone to meet him in Arizona, where he bilked her out of her retirement savings. She'd called Jim, who bought her a plane ticket. He picked her up at the airport in the city. That's where he'd gone the day I stopped by Stone. Jim promoted Miss Taylor to personnel director since that person had retired. I hoped her first order of business would be to fire Mia.

"Her mother and sister must be so relieved," I said. "Miss Taylor's story has a happy ending, sort of, if you don't count losing your life savings."

"What's money, really? She's safe and back home, and that's all that really matters."

"Says the man with the good-paying job," I said.

He chuckled. Before I hung up, I told him I was heading to the cabin and would be back to Three Rivers later that evening and that I hoped to have a chance to talk with Miss Taylor soon. I wanted to lay to rest those rumors about her and Billy. Nothing had gone on between them. I was sure of it. Still, there were those lunches.

Before I headed back up the highway, I called Stella. She answered on the first ring.

"Mackenzie, I can't talk now. I'm just heading out."

"Will it be okay for me to stop by and pick up the, um, package later?"

She paused. "Yes, I'll be back around six if that works for you."

"Great," I said. "By the way, Stella, I had Billy's prescription bottle at the motel the other night. Any idea what happened to it?"

She paused, longer this time. *Oh. I know that she knows that I know.* Clever Me was proud.

Stella cleared her throat. "I, uh, noticed it was there and wanted to get it checked, just in case."

"And did you?"

"Yes! Gordon at the pharmacy said it was antacid medication. Oh, Mackenzie, I was so worried it was going to be something bad. I was just so relieved!"

Okay, so Stella the Worried Mother had taken the bottle to test her theory that her son was sober. I couldn't be mad at her for doing exactly what I was planning to do.

"That's a relief, Stella. Seems you were right. Billy—er, William—was sober." I wasn't absolutely certain that was the case, but I wanted to get going. I told her I'd see her at six and disconnected.

Miss Taylor? Mystery solved. Prescription bottle? Ditto. So far, so good.

I pulled into the driveway of the cabin with maybe an hour of daylight left. Billy's note had said, "Good time. Memories like a warm blanket." The note had irked me. *Good time, Billy? Just one?* But now I knew he was hinting about the clock. *Duh. Time? Clock? Way to pick up on a clue, Mackenzie.* Snarky Me really needed to shut up. If that was a clue, it was a pretty lame one.

Back at the crawl space, I stooped down, shining my little flashlight under the cabin. No sign of critters, but the skunk stench remained. I got down on my belly and started the low crawl in, holding the mini flashlight between my teeth, ignoring the irritation in my still-tender kneecaps.

The large lump I'd seen the other day lay ahead. What was it doing there? I paused, took the mini flashlight out of my mouth, and whistled softly—in case the guard skunk was skulking behind it. No eyes appeared. Nobody hissed. And the lump didn't move.

I inched closer and tapped the lump with the flashlight. No movement, just a hollow clunk. I inched closer and touched it with my hand. Cloth. A blanket, maybe? I pulled the cloth and the lump toward me and scooted backward out of the crawl space, dragging it along.

Out from under the cabin, I set the bundle down on the front steps. I swiped at the cobwebs and dirt on my face and arms, then sat and unwrapped the fabric—an old army blanket I recognized from our camping days. The olive drab, scratchy wool smelled strongly of skunk and was wrapped around the old clock that Stella thought I stole.

Good time, warm blanket? Billy should have said, "Ugly clock. Skunky blanket."

I muttered aloud, "Dammit, Billy! You had this all along and let your mother blame me for stealing it? What the hell?"

I looked at the clock. Still hideous. And yes, we had a key we used to wind it, just so it would work when Stella and Jim visited. A key that I figured was lost. The key Billy left for me.

I turned the clock around and opened the back. A little envelope was tucked inside. I opened it and found another note from Billy. "This explains everything." I shook the contents of the envelope into my palm. A flash drive. If Billy did have "something on somebody," as his buddy Walter suggested, it would be on this memory stick, I was certain. And I was sure Ben Marks would want to check it out.

I put the note and the flash drive into my jeans pocket. I shoved the blanket back under the cabin—I didn't want it stinking up my car—and set the clock on Charlotte's back seat. As an afterthought, I buckled the seat belt around the clock.

Heaven forbid I should have an accident and break you, you ugly old thing, before I can return you to Stella.

Next stop: Stella's. Return the clock, get the money. Then go see Ben Marks, give him the flash drive, and see what secrets it holds. I got into the car, plugged my cell into the car charger, and stuck the mini flashlight back in the glove compartment. I put the key into the ignition, but before I started Charlotte, I decided I needed one more thing.

I got out and walked to the front of the cabin, wanting one more goodbye to the past, to Billy. The sun was setting across the lake, turning the water burnished gold. I spent a moment, eyes closed, letting warm memories flow over me. Then, taking one last breath of lake air, I whispered, "Goodbye, Billy."

As I turned to leave, I noticed that the cabin door stood open. It had been closed when I arrived. Maybe Amanda had returned to finish cleaning. I took one step toward the cabin, and that's as far as I got. On the periphery of my vision, I caught a quick movement to my left, and then something hit me on the back of my head. Hard. Very, very hard.

I've always wondered if you really see stars when someone conks you on the head. You do. I saw the stars, then everything went black.

CHAPTER THIRTY-THREE

I CAME TO, SITTING IN the dirt outside the cabin. Tied to a tree with rope. Mouth taped shut. My wrists were duct-taped together and taped around my knees. Any more tape, and I'd have looked like a silver mummy. The base of my skull throbbed.

The sun had set, and darkness was descending fast. I looked toward the cabin. The front door stood open. In the fading light, I saw a figure moving quickly inside the structure. I heard breaking glass and the thump of furniture being thrown, all accompanied by a barrage of curse words. Whoever it was, was destroying the cabin and would likely try to destroy me next.

I've heard people say that thing about life "flashing before you" when you think you're going to die. That didn't happen for me. No scenes from childhood. No images of family. Only anger.

I was too young to die. I'd never had a baby, not that I wanted one, but I didn't want the possibility of having one taken away by somebody else. I'd never been to New York. I'd never eaten dim sum, whatever that was.

Maybe I didn't see any flashes because I knew I wasn't going to let anybody keep me from tasting exotic Chinese food. In New York City.

Heart pounding, I stretched forward and pulled my knees toward my face. I heard Tansy in yoga class, "Breathe in, and with the out breath, stretch just a little farther."

Calm yourself, Rational Me whispered. *Focus.* Breathing in through my nose, breathing out. With each exhale, stretching a little more, drawing knees closer. Willing my body to go beyond what I thought it was capable of. *Just a little more. A little more!* On the fifth breath, my fingers were close enough to rip the duct tape from my mouth. *Yeow! So long mustache hairs!*

I glanced toward the cabin. The destruction continued.

Curling forward again, I chewed at the tape around my wrists. *Come on! Come on!* Several violent bites and my hands broke free. I ripped the rest of the tape away. The rope was all that held me now.

Slide down! Slide down! Whichever part of me was helping was smart. I slid down under the rope, wriggled it over my head, and I was free.

I stood up, dizzy, just as someone backed out of the cabin, sloshing liquid from a blue container. I caught the smell—not gasoline, but kerosene. I'd smelled it before, years ago, when Gram had a kerosene oil lamp. I smelled it again the night of the apartment fire.

The person in the cabin lit one of those propane lighter sticks, held it aloft a moment, and then, delicately, almost reverently, touched it to the liquid. The stream whooshed into flame, and within seconds the entire cabin was engulfed. Standing silhouetted against the fire, I recognized Andy, the waitress. Wearing a black hoodie. Her nose ring glinted in the firelight. She stood watching the flames, as if mesmerized, and so did I.

Then, as she turned to the side, I saw in the firelight that the pregnant belly was gone. Then it clicked. When I asked Box about her, he'd said, "Don't believe everything you hear or see."

In a flash, I put a theory together. She'd faked the pregnancy. Had she tried to get Billy to marry her? Maybe Billy rejected her, and she killed him. A woman scorned, hell's fury and all that. Why was she torching the cabin? Was there evidence there? Too late now.

And if she'd killed Billy, she wouldn't hesitate to kill me too. *Get out of here!* I started toward Charlotte just as Andy noticed me. "What the hell—?" she yelled and came out of the cabin, fast.

No time to get to my car. I ran toward the road, yelling back as I ran. "You faked it! You killed him!"

She let out a shrill laugh. "No shit, Sherlock! You figured it out!"

The cornfield lay ahead. I dove into it, shoving stalks aside with my arms, the sharp, brittle leaves like razors against my skin.

My right foot caught on something. I went down hard, leaves and stalks poking and tearing at my hands and face, dust and dirt clogging my mouth and nose. I tasted blood. I'd bitten my lip.

I scrambled to my feet.

Pain shot through my right ankle and up into my shin.

A sprain? A break?

Keep moving! Cry later!

The pain slowed me, but I thrashed onward, hoping she wouldn't follow. I wasn't thinking, really, just pushing myself forward toward, I hoped, the road.

After a minute or two of limping and struggling, I slowed to catch my breath. My side ached, my head throbbed. I listened. No one thrashing. Had she given up?

I smelled it before I saw the smoke rising behind me.

Flames devoured the dry cornstalks, like a prairie fire in August. I picked up my pace, fighting forward.

Toward freedom or death? I couldn't be sure.

The smoke thickened. The wind had picked up and was at my back, coming off the lake, driving the smoke and flames closer.

Lungs burning, heart pounding, adrenaline fueling me, I stumbled on and finally collapsed onto my belly in a small clearing at the far edge of the cornfield. My ankle throbbed, my head hurt, my knees stung. My nose and throat burned from the smoke, thicker and closer now.

Get up! Run to the road! Rational Me ordered.

I wasn't sure I could.

I pulled myself to all fours, trying to gather strength to move forward, when Andy called out in a sing-songy tone, "Sherrrrlock . . . come out, come out wherever you are." The taunt came from my right side, repeated, closer and closer.

I lay perfectly still, like a child who hides herself and closes her eyes, figuring you can't see her since she can't see you. I didn't want to move until I was sure where Andy was.

Then directly in front of me, I heard, "There you are."

I raised my head to see the beam of a flashlight playing across the ground of the clearing. How had Andy gotten here so fast? The field had seemed larger in the daylight. And I'd been hobbling and thrashing through the corn, while Andy was moving at full capacity alongside the field to where she figured I'd come out. She wasn't pregnant, and I was wounded. I'd misjudged her and the cornfield.

I lay in the dirt, panting, my ankle shooting sharp darts of pain up through my shin.

Trapped.

Then I heard a male voice. Cold. Flat. Determined. "Get up, or I'll kill you right there in the dirt."

I raised myself up and sat back on my heels. The pressure on my ankle eased the pain a little bit. In the firelight, Eric Boxleitner pointed a gun at me. And the look on his face told me he was prepared to use it.

I figured I'd get some answers before I died. "Were you ever pregnant, Andy?"

"Nope," she said with a chuckle. "I said I wanted everyone to be surprised. So. Surprise!"

She laughed again. I fake laughed. This was going very well. We were becoming friends.

I looked at Box. "Before you shoot me, would it be okay if you told me why you killed Billy? I'll take it to my grave, I promise." I was stalling for time. The fire was getting closer, and pretty soon, we'd all have to move. I'd be able to get away then.

Andy laughed. "*He* didn't do it! He's an idiot! All *he* did was steal the Special K from my sister's clinic—"

Box yelled, "Shut up!" He lunged toward her.

She dodged, yelled, "No, you shut up, you stupid piece of shit!" She grabbed the gun from his hand and shoved him to the ground. Stronger than she looked. Box sat down hard, then crab-walked backward a few feet away.

Andy turned back to me. "*I* did it! *I* gave Billy the ketamine, and then I shot him up with heroin. We used to do that before he got clean. He never knew what hit him."

I felt the white flame of rage in my chest. I wanted to jump up and strangle her. I fought for control, buying time as the fire got closer. "Why, Andy? Why did you do it?"

"You want to know why? Because I told him I loved him, and he just said, 'Okay.' And when I said I was pregnant, he said, 'Get rid of it!' What a bastard!"

"I can't believe he said that!" I said but thought, *Can't blame you if you did, Billy.*

Andy talked faster, gun in one hand, flashlight in the other, waving both and shouting. "My father thinks I'm a total loser! My perfect sister Kim is married. Has kids! Little Miss Perfect veterinarian with her perfect little life! Why can't I have that?"

Crying, she screamed at me. "Why? Why not me? Oh, because I'm just such a terrible sinner? That's what my stepfather says, Mr. Perfect Holy Man! I hate him! He's the reason I started using to begin with!"

My mind snapped to the connections: What had Stella said? Daughters of the pastor—the veterinarian, Kimberly, Stella said. And the other daughter. What was the name? Kassie? Kassandra probably, then Andy for short. Sanders, her mother's last name. The black sheep, Stella had said.

Andy—Kassandra—kept shouting and waving the gun around. Eric, back on his feet, tried to grab her arm.

She yelled, "Hey!" and shoved him away again.

I flashed back to hearing her shout, "Hey!" just before she'd pushed me down. I remembered then, the sun's glint off her nose ring in the sun as she ran down the alley. Hoodie Guy wasn't a guy at all. But I would never have suspected a pregnant waitress of stalking me.

I heard the crackle of cornstalks burning behind me. The smoke intensified as the wind increased, driving the flames closer. We were all going to be roasted if I didn't do something.

I talked fast, shouting, "Billy should have married you! You're smart and funny and pretty . . ."

Her face twisted and she yelled, "Oh really? No way he'd ever marry me. You know why?"

I shook my head.

She screamed, "I'll tell you why. Because he still loved you. He told me he wanted to get clean, so you'd take him back! He. Loved. You!"

"It was you stalking me in Three Rivers!"

She laughed. "Yes! I watched you. I wanted to find out why Billy thought you were so damn special. But you're not. You're just an ordinary—you should have died in that fire!"

I heard a click-click as she cocked the gun. Jesus, it was probably Billy's gun. I closed my eyes and folded over, lowering my forehead to the ground.

Life went into slow motion. I saw Gram's face. This was it.

And then it happened.

I heard rustling and sensed a stirring all around me, then the tickle of tiny feet scurrying up my back, over my neck, through my squirrelly hair, accompanied by a million little squeaks. Field mice. Hundreds—maybe thousands—of field mice running to escape the fire.

A second later, they reached Andy. She shrieked, dropped the gun and the flashlight, and threw herself at Box. He stumbled backward, shoved her aside, and ran toward the road.

Andy screeched and jumped frantically, yelling, "HELP ME! HELLLLLP ME! Get . . . them . . . OFF MEEEE!"

I heard sirens approaching. I scrambled to my feet, ran toward her, grabbed her, and channeling every ounce of my remaining strength, drove my right fist into her face. "That's for Billy!"

She landed hard on her backside. Mice kept coming, swarming over her legs and arms. She struggled to her feet, and, swatting at mice and screaming, ran toward the road.

I picked up the flashlight, found the gun, and held it at arm's length, my pinky in the trigger guard. I hobbled after Andy, wiggling and jiggling to dislodge the mice crawling on me. *Ewwww.*

Andy ran out onto the road, right into the path of a squad car. It stopped inches from hitting her. *Bummer!* Snarky Me thought. Or maybe Snarky yelled it out loud.

I limped toward the road and away from the burning field as fast as I could move—just as more flashing lights and sirens came around the bend. Someone had reported the fire. In a moment, floodlights from the firetrucks illuminated the scene as firefighters hustled to extinguish the flames.

Ben Marks got out of the squad car, and Andy threw herself into his arms, screaming and sobbing that he had to save her because I was trying to kill her.

"Not true, Ben!" I shouted and limped toward him, hands above my head just in case he believed her. Eric Boxleitner was nowhere in sight, probably hightailing it into the next county.

Ben put Andy in the back of the squad car, "For your own protection," he told her, "while I get to the bottom of this."

With Andy secured and the gun safely in his possession, Ben stood with me at the side of the road as I told him what I knew, how Andy had faked her pregnancy to try to trap Billy into marriage. How she'd admitted she'd killed him with a drug overdose.

In the middle of my story, Andy pounded on the window of the squad car, yelling. Ben opened the door, and she said, "It was all Eric's idea! He stole the ketamine from my sister's clinic. He said Billy wouldn't feel a thing, that we should drug him and then take the money!"

"What money?" Ben asked.

"We knew Billy had a bunch of cash in the cabin. But we couldn't find it!"

Ben turned to me. "Do you know anything about this money?"

I shrugged. I didn't want to say anything since I wasn't sure where the money came from. Andy went on, spilling her guts, telling Ben that Box said they should burn the cabin just to destroy any evidence that might be there.

Ben interrupted her. "Okay, okay, you can tell me the whole story back at the station."

Andy crossed her arms and slumped back against the seat, shooting me a look that said she was sorry she hadn't finished me off when she had the chance.

I told Ben how I'd been outside the cabin when she got there, how someone—probably Box—had knocked me out and tied me to a tree. How they chased me and set the cornfield on fire. It all came rushing out.

Then Ben noticed my ankle, the contusion on the back of my head, my black eye, and the dirt and blood congealing in the cuts on my face, arms, and hands.

"I'm fine," I said. He didn't believe me. He waved a paramedic over to us. "This is Janine. She'll take you to Our Lady of Mercy in Three Rivers." I protested. Ben insisted as he looped his left arm around me and pulled my right arm around his neck. With Janine supporting me on the other side, I hobbled to the ambulance. I refused to ride in the back.

Ben laid a blanket over my lap and buckled me in. As he was about to close the door, I said, "Wait! My car is back there at the cabin. The keys are in it, and so is my cell!" *OMG. Life without a cell phone? Will I survive?* "Maybe someone could get it out of there before it gets incinerated?"

He looked toward the cabin. "Might be too late for that, but I'll see what we can do."

I remembered the flash drive and dug it, painfully, from my jeans pocket. "Billy left this. Maybe you can figure out what's on it?"

Ben took it. "I'll let you know what I find." He looked me in the eyes then, holding my gaze a little longer than I would expect from casual acquaintances. He picked a piece of cornstalk from my hair, then cleared his throat. "I'm—uh—glad you're okay. I'll be in touch."

He shut the door, and Janine turned the ambulance around. I closed my eyes as we drove through the night toward Three Rivers while Janine kept up a constant conversation, reminding me to stay awake.

If Gram had been there, she'd have been checking me for wonky eyeballs.

CHAPTER THIRTY-FOUR

Thursday, November 1
All Saints' Day

I SPENT TUESDAY NIGHT AND most of Wednesday—Halloween—being "observed" at Our Lady of Mercy. A major portion of that time, Gram was doing the observing.

Late Tuesday night, the rain had come, at last, a glorious deluge that ended our drought, swamped the streets, and caused the Wolf River to rise. Basements in downtown buildings flooded, including Lou's. She called Gram to say I wouldn't need to start working there for another week or so.

Fine with me. I needed time to recover. I had a hell of a bump on the back of my head and an angry bruise on my cheek. Scraping my face through the cornfield had added a zillion little scratches and nicks. A nurse had cleaned me up, but I was going to have scabs galore. My ankle—just sprained, not broken—looked twice its normal size, encircled by a wicked-looking purplish bruise. And my hair, still recovering from the mistimed dye job, was a fright. I could have gone trick-or-treating *sans* costume.

By late afternoon on Halloween, the doctor had cleared me to go home. I called my mother to let her know, got dressed, and sat on the edge of the bed, reading my discharge instructions while I waited for my mom.

I heard a rap on the open door and looked up at Ben Marks smiling at me. "Can I come in?"

My hand went to my cheek. "Aw, geez. I look awful," I said.

He walked toward me, looking good—very good—in jeans and a Deerwood PD-logoed dark blue windbreaker. Which brought out his very blue eyes. Not that I noticed.

"You look fine." He glanced at the top of my head. "And cornstalk free."

I raked a hand through my hair. "I'm a mess."

"You're alive."

"Barely," I said.

He smiled and looked at me. Really looked. The only word I can think of to describe that look is "unsettling." Like how I imagine it would feel to be in an earthquake. Snarky Me piped up. *Ooh, baby, I felt the earth move! What a cliché!*

Snarky was right. I would have kicked myself, but I didn't need any more pain.

After a moment, Ben broke eye contact, cleared his throat, and shifted into cop mode. Looking at his phone, he said, "I checked on your car. Sorry, but it's a total loss." He reached into his jacket pocket, then handed me my cell and charging cord. "It's a miracle these made it. So did that thing on the back seat, I think. It may have some damage."

I asked him to please take "that thing" back to Stella. "She'll be thrilled."

Ben said a friend of his could tow the car to Boxleitner's junkyard, but I couldn't bear the thought of Box's father's grubby paws touching Charlotte. "Maybe your friend could tow it here?"

Ben agreed. Charlotte had served me well and deserved a decent send-off.

"What about that flash drive? Anything there?" I asked.

Ben nodded. "I've uploaded the contents. It's evidence, so I can't give you a copy, but I thought you'd want to see it. Okay if I sit?"

I nodded. He sat next to me. He smelled like a forest full of sunshine and fresh air. *Get a grip*, Snarky said. *Hush*, I said.

Ben opened a video file on his phone and held it so we both could see.

Billy. I was looking at a ghost. The last time I'd seen him, he hadn't been talking, or even breathing. But here he was, alive and well and looking into the camera. I squeezed my eyes shut against a swell of tears and made a little strangled sound.

Ben paused the video. "You doing okay?"

I cleared my throat. My voice strained, I said, "It's just . . . hard to . . ." Then I couldn't hold back. The tears flowed. Ben put an arm around me, pulled me toward himself. I leaned into his chest and cried against his jacket.

After several minutes, I pulled away, grabbed a tissue from the bedside box, wiped my face, and blew my nose. I looked at Ben. I had to be quite the sight, all scratched and scabby, puffy and red.

I pointed at his jacket. "Sorry about the wet spot there."

Ben smiled. "Not a problem. The jacket's seen worse. You think you're ready to watch now?" I swallowed and nodded. He restarted the video.

Billy stated his name, the date, and the time. In good cop form. "I'm creating this video as my testimony," he said. He had proof that his uncle Eddie faked the results of the trials with the invention that had made him rich. Two people died, and Eddie covered that up. He'd paid off the families and then sold the patent for millions to his former employer.

All the evidence—the falsified research data, payoffs to the families—was on the flash drive. Where Billy got all this, he didn't say.

Billy admitted in the video that he'd been blackmailing Eddie but had started to feel guilty about the whole thing. He tried to convince Eddie to speak up before anyone else got hurt.

The video ended with Billy saying, "I'm leaving this video testimony and the evidence, just in case something happens to me." Something did, but not what Billy had anticipated. Eddie didn't kill him; Andy and Box got there first.

As Ben put the phone into his pocket, I thought a silent, last goodbye to the sweet boy I once knew.

"He did the right thing, leaving this," Ben said.

Well done, Billy. I blew my nose again and let out a sigh. "Has Eddie been arrested?"

"Nope. He's gone, probably someplace without an extradition treaty, so we can't ask him about all this. But his wife had plenty to tell us." Ben told me that Amanda, realizing Eddie had left her to the wolves, was more than happy to tell the police what she knew.

Eddie, when he was drunk after the funeral, told Amanda that Billy needed to be silenced. The week before Billy died, Eddie had gone to the cabin and stuffed rags into the stove chimney, waiting for Billy to light a fire and die of carbon monoxide. Eddie figured everyone would assume it was an accident or suicide.

"A ridiculously inefficient way to try to kill someone, to say the least," Ben said.

Amanda, horrified, had gone to the cabin to remove the rags; that explained the dirt smudges on her face when we met in the driveway. She wasn't there to clean the cabin. She was there cleaning up after her sleazeball husband.

I said, "And the weather had been so warm, Billy never lit the stove. But he would have eventually. It was just a matter of time." I shuddered.

"But he didn't, and we have confessions from Kassandra Sanders and Eric Boxleitner. Eric turned himself in after a friend of Billy's named Joe Chastain, um, *persuaded* him to do so."

I smiled at that. *Way to go, Joe.*

Ben continued. "We have Eric on security footage for some of those break-ins, including the vet clinic. They're both facing multiple charges, including arson and attempted murder."

"*Attempted?* They *admitted* that they *murdered* Billy!"

"They insist they didn't mean to. We'll see. Regardless, they're both facing serious jail time. And the mystery is solved. You were right; I'm glad you trusted your intuition. Good job."

I nodded. He cleared his throat and looked at me again. Unsettling, indeed. "Okay if I call you sometime? Maybe go out?" I nodded again. What was it about this guy that made me go mute?

He stood to leave, then said, "Oh, I almost forgot. I have something for you from Helen Taylor." He reached into his jacket and handed me an envelope with my first name written on it in perfect penmanship.

I found my voice, finally. "Thanks for everything, Ben."

He smiled. I liked his smile a lot. "I'll call you," he said and left.

Inside the envelope were a sympathy card and a handwritten letter. Miss Taylor offered her condolences, then wrote:

"I'm writing to put your mind at ease. Billy and I were good friends. He talked about you often, how bright and beautiful you were, and how he regretted hurting you." I felt a pang of sadness at that. She went on to say that she'd overheard discussions between Jim and Eddie in the office with "intimations of impropriety on Eddie's part." She told Billy "since he'd been in law enforcement." She said she was glad he'd found evidence, adding, "Thanks to you, the police have it now. Perhaps justice will be done."

She closed with, "I hope this letter brings you a modicum of peace. Billy was a wonderful young man, and he loved you very much. Yours sincerely, Helen Taylor."

A wave of emotion swamped me, sadness mixed with relief and gratitude. Miss Taylor was one fine person, and I was glad she was okay.

BACK AT THE VICTORIAN, I LIMPED up the stairs, with Gram on one side and my mother behind me, to the Rose Room, where I ensconced myself in the big pink bed.

Mom and Gram fussed over me as I dozed off and on, popping over-the-counter pain medication and icing my ankle. My mom took my dirty clothes to wash them, holding them at arm's length. "These smell like a fire. Twice in one week, Mackenzie? Honestly!"

"Yeah, yeah," I muttered. "I'll try not to get incinerated again, Mom."

"Well, I do hope you'll be more careful. You never know," she said. I was too tired to argue.

I hobbled downstairs to the dining room on Thursday morning, where I found Gram and my mother having coffee at the big mahogany table. Gram was reading *The Bull*, wearing a pink velour jogging suit—no doubt another fabulous find from Lou's. I assumed Nathan was still in bed. My mother, working on the sudoku, wore black leggings and her Three Rivers Marathon shirt, her cheeks flushed and forehead glistening.

"How was your run, Mom?"

"Great! I love mornings like this, the cool fresh air after a rain. Everything was so dry and dusty out there, and now it's like the whole town has been washed clean."

The doorbell rang. My mom answered and returned to the dining room carrying a huge—as in ginormous—arrangement of roses, along with a get-well card from Tansy. The card included a promise of a dozen free yoga sessions for all of us—me, Gram, my mother. Also a gift certificate to her fancy-shmancy hair salon in the city. Guaranteed to rid me of all traces of squirrel. Best. Friend. Ever.

"Mackenzie, listen to this!" Gram said. "You made the paper!" She read aloud how the fire Tuesday night near Deerwood had spread from where I was and burned a couple thousand acres of forest and fields and more than a dozen lake homes. I wondered if the remains of Maxwell's store had survived. Probably not.

Fortunately, no one died. The volunteers in Deerwood got help from firefighters from several surrounding counties before it was finally contained. And then, after midnight, a heavy rain had drowned any remaining hot spots.

"The fire made the paper, not me," I said.

They asked me to tell the story again of Billy and Andy and the cornfield. I'd tried to tell them when they came to the hospital, but I wasn't 100 percent coherent there. I told them what I remembered.

"So, this Andy faked being pregnant, thinking she could force Billy to marry her?" Gram asked.

My mother scoffed. "Seriously? Seems ridiculous nowadays. Who cares about getting married anymore?"

Gram shook her head. "Kids these days. Honestly. But what did you say about a veterinary clinic? Keta—what? What's that?"

"Ketamine. It's an animal tranquilizer," my mother said. "Don't ask me how I know."

We both shot her a look, and I went on. "Andy claimed she and Billy did that all the time—she called it Special K—and said she had no idea he was going to die. But Eric Boxleitner is telling a different story, how they decided to do it together, then planned to steal Billy's money and leave town."

"Horrible. Just horrible," Gram said. "Who does something like that?"

"Oh, Mother, don't be so naïve. The world is an awful place these days," my mother said, then looked at me. "Wait. Billy's money? What money?"

I ignored her. The money was still sitting in Stella's safe until I could figure out what to do. Until then, I wasn't going to discuss it, especially with my mother. I changed the subject. "It turns out Andy was the one who was stalking me," I said.

Gram and my mom gave me startled looks, and my mother spoke, "What do you mean *stalking*?"

I filled them in, then concluded my tale. "It was an overdose, all right, but Billy didn't do it. He was, indeed, clean and sober. Stella and Jim must be relieved," I said.

And she must be delighted to have the clock back. Snarky Me was alive and well.

A moment of silence as they digested the story, and then my mother looked at me. "So, how many mice do you think there were?" *Seriously? I almost got burned alive—twice—and could have been shot to death, and my mother wants to know how many mice there were?*

I paused. "Um, ten thousand four hundred and twenty-three." I winked at Gram.

"Twenty-four," she said, winking back, "and a half."

My mother reddened and frowned at us. "Okay, fine. You two don't have to be so smart." She gave a little shiver and rubbed her arms. "Ugh. I hate those nasty little buggers." She got up and went into the kitchen.

Gram reached over and patted my arm. "I hate mice too, but I love the ones who saved your life." She looked at me tenderly. "When I think about what could have happened . . ."

I covered her hand with mine. "But it didn't happen, Gram. I'm okay. Everything is okay now. Mice are fine as long as they don't run up my pant legs." I wiggled my fingers against Gram's arm. Her turn to shiver.

My mother returned to the table with the coffee pot. She poured a refill into Gram's World's Best Grandma mug, then held the pot toward me. "You, Mackenzie?"

I covered my half-full mug with my hand. "No thanks, Mom. I'm fine."

I leaned back in the dining room chair, holding my warm coffee mug against my sore cheek, listening to Gram's sweet voice as she read aloud. "Looks like Lambert's has a sale on ground chuck this week. Sweet potatoes too. Time to start getting ready for Thanksgiving." Life goes on.

I sighed, content, sipping my coffee. I looked out the big bay window at the intensely blue, clear November sky and watched as the morning sun cast a rainbow through the stained-glass panel above the window.

Billy was gone forever, but thanks to him, I had some financial security, at least for now. Meanwhile, I had a part-time job at Lou's Vintage to keep me busy—as soon as she bailed out her basement.

In the romance department, Kyle was history. Bangladesh and Peter Pan were welcome to him. But I had one, two, or maybe even three potentials. Frank? Vince? Ben? Who knew how things might play out? And I knew that, if none of them worked out, I'd be okay by myself.

I had my family. I had my friends. And for now, I had a roof over my head, a cozy place to sleep, and an unlimited supply of hugs. And cookies.

At that moment, I felt deep satisfaction at having found answers for Billy, for myself, and for the other people who cared about him. That felt noble, with justice being done. Bad people were in jail, and I'd helped make that happen.

I rubbed my knuckles, where they'd connected with Andy's face. Satisfying, yes.

I felt something else too. What was it? I'd taken chances, nosed around, poked the beehive, risked my life. And in all of that, I'd felt a rush of adrenaline, a surge of strength, and a sense of empowerment.

I could have been incinerated. Shot. Dead. And part of me loved it.

Gram taught us kids: "Say yes when something scares you." Face your fear. Take action. If I ignore Anxious Me's fretting, Brave Me says yes when I'm scared.

And, evidently, when I'm terrified out of my skull, Brave Me becomes Badass Me and says, "Hell, yeah!"

If Mackenzie Prentice and her inner committee made you smile, I'd be so grateful if you left a quick review. A sentence or two from you helps other readers discover the series and means more to me than you might imagine.

With deep gratitude,

Mary

BURIED IN TREASURE

Book Two in the Mackenzie Prentice Mysteries

MACKENZIE PRENTICE HAS SWORN OFF SNOOPING into other people's business, but when a family friend dies, her grandmother has a feeling something's just not right. She asks Mack to check things out, ask a few questions, see if there's anything amiss. And when Gram asks you to do something, there's really no point in refusing. You just do it.

Mack loves a good puzzle almost as much as she loves her grandmother. That's how she finds herself BURIED IN TREASURE, nosing around in a hoard of mystery and intrigue. She's sure the answers she seeks are concealed somewhere in the massive pile of stuff—football heroes and bird feathers, living things and things that are, most definitely, dead. She puts herself in danger, ignoring the warnings of the echoes from the past, determined to uncover the truth of who did what to whom, when, and why, with an assist from a highly unlikely new friend.

Mackenzie Prentice is thirty-five, has a touch of OCD, is addicted to sugar, may occasionally drink too much, and has those voices in her head commenting on her choices. Her relationship status: single but open to possibilities.

MARY PIERCE is delighted to bring this second book in her new series of Mackenzie Prentice Mysteries.

ACKNOWLEDGMENTS

MACK WAS BORN LONG AGO, IN an upstairs apartment in the inner city, where an eight-year-old Nancy Drew fan dreamed of one day writing her own mystery. The little girl—let's call her Gladys—dreamed poems and stories in her bedroom—a sunporch with seven windows that afforded her a great view of life on the city streets.

Over the years, life wound its way (as life will) through relationships and careers, eventually leading to writing non-fiction articles and books for publication and traveling around the country as a keynote speaker and humorist. Then life took a left turn into caregiving and a surprising new career as a clinical mental health counselor. But the dream of writing mysteries lived on until, finally, Mack came into being in the form you are reading right now.

Thank you, Reader, first and foremost, for inviting Mack into your world. And to the countless friends who have asked, "When is the book coming out?" Well, here she is, and I thank you for your enthusiastic support!

And now it's time to thank the others—so many—who helped along the way.

Thanks to daughter Katy Stevens for her enthusiasm as a reader and for insight into life in a Victorian home. (Listen carefully; you may hear Gram and Nathan in the kitchen.) To daughter Lizz Berry, so much gratitude for helping with research, first readings and suggestions for improvements, and insight into being a tech-savvy thirty-something. Thanks to son, Alex Berry, who asked on a long-ago day, "Mom, who will write your stories if you don't?" (Mack is part of the answer.) And the rest of the gang: Jenny, Laura, Danny, Erin, Keith, Jeff, Chris, Girl Alex, and all the grandkids and grandpups too. Close in my heart, always!

Thanks to my sweet sister and first reader Carol Persons for her encouragement and incredible eye for detail in the first edits. ("Take that comma out, but save it. You'll need it on the next page.") Thanks to fellow writer Fern Brown for being the first to read the complete book and for so much encouragement along the way. (Is Mack wearing jeans or sweats? Still not sure!)

A huge thank you to editor, coach, book designer, and consultant Michelle Rayburn (missionandmedia.com). Thank you for the gorgeous design and your brilliant editing down to the last comma. (I'll never look at an ellipsis the same way and will likely still get it wrong!) I so appreciate your constant encouragement, patience, and massive knowledge about all things publishing. We simply wouldn't be here without you, Michelle.

Thanks to graphic designer Geri Krause (gerikrause.com) for the stunning cover art. You are so very gifted, my friend, and a blessing in my life!

Thanks to Joe Coughlin for insight into police matters;

nothing quite like that voice of authority. Thanks for being so patient with my civilian questions.

Thanks to Nick Butler and other members of the Chippewa Valley Writers Guild, who gave such honest feedback and helped me see where I was holding back. You were right, I was wrong, and Mack is more authentic because of you. (You made her cry!)

If we could send gratitude "through the veil," I'd thank my late father, lover of words and music, who always believed, always encouraged, and carried Gladys's poems in his wallet until they fell apart.

Finally, as always, thank you, my darling Terry, for a lifetime of cheerleading and encouragement. Because of your unflinching support of all things creative, Mack lives. And so do I.

ABOUT THE AUTHOR

MARY PIERCE IS THE AUTHOR OF three books of humorous inspiration published by Zondervan/Harper Collins: *When Did I Stop Being Barbie and Become Mrs. Potato Head*; *Confessions of a Prayer Wimp*; and *When Did My Life Become a Game of Twister.*

Mary spent the better part of twenty years writing for publication—books, articles, and a humor column for a national magazine—and as a speaker/humorist, traveling around the country bringing laughter and encouragement to audiences at women's wellness events and retreats.

She left the speaking circuit to care for her aging mother, who had dementia. After six years as a primary family caregiver, Mary returned to school, earning a Master of Science degree in Clinical Mental Health Counseling at the age of sixty. As a counselor/psychotherapist, she works with adults in transition who are dealing with depression, anxiety, and life changes. She specializes in trauma reprocessing and caregiver support, as well as grief support.

In the other half of her time, she writes—the Mackenzie Prentice mystery series and other projects. She also enjoys messing around with collage and assemblage as a mixed-media artist. (What is it about fingers full of paint and glue that brings such joy?)

She and her husband, Terry, share six children and eleven grandchildren. They make their home in Wisconsin with a West Highland "terrorist" named Zoey, and Sammy, a goldendoodle puppy named after their favorite pizza place.

Visit Mary at marypierceauthor.com.

www.ingramcontent.com/pod-product-compliance
Lightning Source LLC
Chambersburg PA
CBHW032043240626
47154CB00003B/1050